# Rescued

By

## Caroline McKinley

Cover art by

Edited by

## Denna Holm

Published by

Crimson Cloak Publishing

Copyright © 2016

ISBN 13: 978-1-68160-174-8

ISBN 10:   1-68160-174-5

Publishers Publication in Data

*McKinley, Caroline*
*Rescued*
1. Family Problems  2. High School Students  3. Rescue Dogs
4. Coming of Age  5. Human-animal Relationships
6.  Friendship  7. Young Adult Fiction

I was ordered by the Riverton Juvenile Court to report to the Town Animal Shelter at *precisely* 3:30 on the last Friday before summer break. It didn't leave me much time. I really wanted to talk to my teacher since it was his last day as well. You would think the justice system would take exception to my being a bit late. I was spending time with faculty, not in the smoking area trying to look cool. I didn't feel cool, and pretending wouldn't get me there. My emotions always seemed to mess me up somehow.

I was in need of some words of literary wisdom before the lights in his classroom went off for good. Mr. Davis' much needed retirement, and freedom, would begin at the same time mine was ending. After almost forty years of driving his love of reading and story through a hailstorm of budget cuts and political headwinds, Mr. D. had had it. His fishing pole and cabin up in Maine were calling. When she was at GW High, my sister Patty took all of his classes. She came home with his book suggestions that went beyond the curriculum, like *Bruiser* and *Little Brother*. And after exhausting the worn out summer reading list, he gave me *A Room on Lorelei Street* and *Chains*. I'm sure I'm not alone when I say the novels really spoke to me. These were tough, sensitive girls with a mission.

I wanted to have a mission, and the writing chops to talk about it.

Mr. D. looked weathered, especially around the eyes. He had this habit of rubbing his temples, as if he had a migraine, which only added to his scholarly charm. It reminded me of those grainy photos of the giants among storytellers, like Ernest Hemingway and John Steinbeck— cigarette in hand, hunched over a typewriter, creating line after line of narrative— only to scratch each one out with dramatic dissatisfaction.

Fifteen minutes before the class ended, we were talking about the use of "irony" in *Catcher in the Rye*. Like Holden Caufield, I had always been frustrated at the phoniness of people in my town and school. As our discussion grew, it became clear that good old Holden was pretty phony himself. So now, as I raced down the road to our town animal shelter, equipped with what I thought was a practical understanding of life's ironies, I thought it *ironic* that my community service had to be forced on me. I mean, isn't that something we should do out of a voluntary desire to help out, not some judicial form of punishment? Not to mention my hundred and fifty hours of forced labor would have to be spent inside cleaning kennels just when the weather had started to warm up after the arctic freeze we scraped through all winter.

Now, before you think otherwise, I am a little nuts for animals. I always wanted a dog, but my parents work pretty long hours. And since I'm always doing some extracurricular gig after school, we thought it would be unfair if we got one and then kept it cooped up in the house, lonely and bored, never having the time to take it out on long walks to sniff around and just be a dog. So, if I had to pick a community service job, being around animals, and dogs in particular, would be my first choice. But to give up my role as Rizzo in the summer musical production of *Grease* made cleaning kennels a whole lot messier. Especially since it was passed on to Sylvia Buchwald, top frenemy (I'll explain why later), who possessed beauty, a killer voice, (though apparently not as good as mine) and parents who were top in their legal and medical fields. She was rich, beautiful, talented, and now had the part I'd dreamed about all year long, not to mention rehearsed in front of my full length mirror, bellowing out notes that would have made all four chairs on the *Voice* turn around. I also lost the rare chance to play alongside a cute Kenickie, who, even rarer, was kind of in to me.

I was handed this sentence due to my intention of sending a "back off" message that got slightly out of control. In the eyes of the judge it was irresponsible and dangerous. So here is how it began, which was, come to think of it, another example of life's ironies.

I was accused of bullying a bully.

Cindy Bender was a junior and a year older. Ever since I knew her, back in elementary, she took pleasure in terrorizing anyone who she believed got in the way of what she wanted—always other girls, pretty girls. One would hope that she had grown out of this by now. It only seemed to have gotten worse. Our school should have employed the philosophy of its namesake, that is, staunch supporter of freedom from tyranny and oppression. But George Washington High was anything but. Another irony. Here I was, standing up for someone's rights against persecution, and I get thrown in the dog house, literally.

Like me, Anna Swenson was a sophomore. Unlike me, she was new to the area after moving up from the city. She had no one to watch her back, except a mother recently widowed, who had to take the first nursing job she could get after her husband died. She was also, unlike me, drop-dead gorgeous and incredibly nice. Our lives connected after my best buddy, Carly McGregor, moved out West with her family. Carly and I had always had a good time together. We never had to explain our actions or remarks. Things were just easy with her. I really missed her. Mr. McGregor was transferred just before school started, so at least we had the summer together. But I wasn't looking forward to starting my sophomore year without her, especially after we shed our tight freshmen skins together. Carly and I were so alike. Anna and I were complete opposites, except when it came to our love of books and music. In fact, that is how we met. We were both cast in the school production of *Oklahoma*. As sophomores it was pretty unusual that we would snag principal roles, but what can I say? We were both that good. She played Laurey, the female lead, and I was her best friend, Ado Annie, who sang *I'm Just a Girl Who Can't say No*. And before you get the wrong idea, 'no' happens to be my favorite word, so definitely no type-casting there.

Anna and I hit it off during rehearsals and had a blast when we performed together. She also hit it off with Cindy Bender's ex, Matt Barkley, who was cast as Curly. Matt sprouted a few tattoos, and also a killer voice. He kind of reminded me of a beefed-up Adam Levine. Underneath all that leather he wore was a song waiting to sing.

Though Matt was clearly interested in Anna beyond their beautiful duets, she felt there was something about him that was a 'little off.' She never went into detail. I never pressed. From what I could tell, he was not her type. Still, she was happy to stay stage friends. She would never intentionally hurt anyone's feelings. That's the kind person she was, just really nice.

I remember when we all took our final bows to a standing ovation. Matt kissed Anna on the cheek and handed her a bouquet of roses. I looked out at the audience and saw Cindy shooting poison darts out of her eyes, aimed right at Anna's heart. This was not good. I didn't want to mention it to her and cause a personal panic in case I'd completely misjudged the situation. I have since learned that my instincts are usually spot on.

The following Monday I was planning on meeting up with Anna to prepare for tryouts for our community theater's summer production of *Grease*. She was a shoo-in for Sandy. Apparently Matt Barkley was going to audition for the role of Danny. I was hoping he wouldn't get it. If he did, that would only give Cindy more ammo to launch her fury. I had a pretty decent shot at Rizzo, but would need to prepare. Not only could Anna sing, but she played a mean piano and was going to teach me a few of the songs, namely "There are worst things I could do." I thought my parents would not be too psyched about my playing the part of a girl who is not only easy with the guys, but thinks she might be pregnant. Knowing how much I wanted the part, not to mention the fact that I was smart enough to avoid becoming the victim of some testosterone inflated ego, 'at least for now,' as my mother said, they gave me the green light.

Anna was down the hall, standing in front of her open locker. As I walked closer, I saw that she was motionless and staring straight inside.

"What's happening?" I asked.

No response. Then when I looked, I understood. Her books, music, leather jacket, sneakers, iPad, and the painting she had completed in art class, were soaking wet. It was must have happened over the weekend, because the smell of mold was powerful.

"What the...? Who would have done this?" I asked stupidly, as if Anna would know. The poor kid was in such shock, she just kept staring until she had to wipe away a few tears. I noticed a note taped to the inside door. Anna had already slid down the wall and sat on the floor, shaking her head in disbelief. "My mother just bought me that iPad."

I pulled the note off the door and headed down the hall to Principle Langdon's office. His door was closed, so I showed the note to his assistant, Mrs. Ford. She read it aloud twice, as if to prove to me she cared.

"*Water for your Roses.* 'Water for your roses?' I don't get it," she said.

"If you were in the audience on Friday, you would," I said rather loudly, because just then Langdon's door opened.

"Would what, Miss Riley?"

"Mr. Langdon, Friday night after the performance of *Oklahoma*—"

"Yes, I was there. Nice job by everyone."

"Yes, thank you, but just now, Anna and I discovered someone flooded her locker over the weekend. Everything, including her new computer, is ruined."

"Oh, no. Where is Anna now?"

"Having a moment of silence."

"And where would that be, Miss Riley?"

"In front of the ruins."

"Mrs. Ford, perhaps you should bring Anna here."

Mrs. Ford left the office shaking her head. "You kids have too much time on your hands."

Speak for yourself, Ford. Between schoolwork, helping my mom out at her struggling real estate business, and rehearsals, I don't have time to search for the best online shopping deals the way you do, as soon as Langdon closes his door. As to what *he* does behind closed doors, I'd rather not think about it.

"What does the vandalism have to do with the performance Friday night?" Langdon asked.

"Well, you probably noticed that Matt gave Anna a bouquet of roses."

"Yes?"

I handed him the note. "Well, take a look at what was taped to her locker door."

"*Water for your roses.* I don't get it."

*Have these people not had their coffee yet?* "Cindy Bender was in the audience."

"Yes?"

"Cindy dated Matt until he broke up with her because of her obsessive compulsive, extreme degree of jealousy over anyone he even looks at."

"All right. I'll talk with Miss Bender, but unless I have proof, I fail to see how we can implicate her. Matt is a popular guy and there could be any number of people who could've got bent out of shape over this."

"'Bent out of shape?' Cindy was spewing out so much toxic energy, I'm surprised the whole auditorium wasn't sealed off."

"I do appreciate your assessment of the situation, but I'll have to do some investigating and talk to the janitorial staff to see if they saw anything suspicious over the weekend, or late that night. Just be patient. We'll get to the bottom of this."

Just then, Anna walked in with Mrs. Ford. Her eyes were swollen and red from crying. She didn't deserve this. Unfortunately, patience was not one of my strengths.

It didn't help that not a soul saw Cindy close to Anna's locker after the show. In fact, Cindy's partner in crime, Sally Peck, swore to Langdon that they were both at Sally's house, babysitting Sally's little brother. Mrs. Peck supported that story, though how she would know for certain is unclear, considering she was at the same school meeting my parents went to. The only other witness would have been Sally's eight-month-old brother, and he wasn't talking.

I n a few weeks, summer would start. That helped Anna put the Bender fear behind her and focus on the summer festival audition for *Grease*. Saturday morning, Anna's mom dropped us off at the community theater before heading over to the hospital for her twelve-hour shift as an ER Nurse. We were both in a pretty awesome mood as we headed through the parking lot singing, *"Grease is the Word,"* at the top of our lungs.

People looked.

We didn't care.

We signed in and got comfortable in the hallway, where about fifty other potentials of all ages and types were waiting. It looked as if it was going to take a few hours to show our stuff, so I decided to head outside and practice a few notes by myself. Anna was a natural and just decided to sit in line by our backpacks with her iPod playing in her ear. After a while, I headed back inside and noticed our bags keeping our place without Anna. There was an older teenage guy sitting next to them. I interrupted him from his meditative lotus pose.

"Excuse me."

He opened his eyes, took his ear bud out and turned off his iPod. It happened to be the same color as Anna's.

"Sorry to interrupt."

"No worries. You looking for your friend?"

"Yeah. Did they call her name already?"

"No. She's using the bathroom. Asked me to watch your stuff and lent me her iPod. I forgot mine. Helps me relax."

"I see that."

"You're Casey, right?"

"Yes, Casey Riley. And you are?"

"Ron, Ron Parrisi. Trying out for the role of Kenickie."

I was sizing up my potential stage love interest. He was pretty cute, in a *just woke up from a nap* sort of way. "Right," I said.

"You know Kenickie, Rizzo's heart throb?" He ran his fingers through long bangs that feathered down the right side of his face and fell into his eye.

"Yes, I know the musical."

"You here to support your friend, or trying out yourself?"

"Both."

"Oh yeah, which part?"

"Rizzo. Kenickie's heart throb."

"Right."

Anna returned, looking a little green.

"Hey, you all right?" I asked

"Yeah, all of a sudden I got really nervous. I guess after all that's happened, I really want this part." She turned to Ron. "Thanks for watching our stuff."

"Hey, thanks for lending me your iPod." To my surprise, he took out an antibacterial "Wet Ones" and wiped off the ear bud. Okay, scruffy but clean. Score one for Kenickie.

"I see you two have met," Anna said.

I was beginning to like the fact that Ron wasn't salivating over Anna, but actually grinning in my direction. And I didn't think it was due to her greenish complexion.

Score two for Kenickie.

"Ron goes to private school up in Massachusetts," Anna said.

Uh, oh. Could be a potential big negative. Was it one of those disciplinarian institutions for juvenile delinquents? Now the ruffled look was beginning to make sense.

"Whereabouts," I asked, about as casually as I could.

"Groton. Just finished my senior year," he replied, even more casually. "Our school lets out a week before Riverton."

Okay, so he's smart, polite, clean and cute, though the bangs falling in his eyes were beginning to make my eyes water. Possibly comes from money, and perhaps thinks I'm cute as well. Score three, four, five, six, and hopefully seven for Kenickie.

"Anna. Anna Swenson," called one of the casting assistants. "You're on deck."

"That's you, girlfriend. Be brilliant," I said.

"Okay, here we go. I'm going to leave my bag here, okay?"

"Yep, yep, we'll watch it." I handed her the water bottle sticking out of her side pocket. "Take this, you may need it."

"Thanks." Anna headed toward the stage. She took a swig of water and choked, her greenish pallor turning fire-engine red. The bottle flew out of her hand as she ran back towards me.

"Water, water," she said through fits of coughing.

I handed her my bottle, which she chugged down in seconds.

"What is it? What's going on?"

Anna just sliced her hand across her throat, like she was done.

"I don't think she can talk right now, Casey," Ron said, noting the obvious. Then he gave her his water bottle, that she also emptied.

"Hot, hot pepper," she said, while fanning her mouth.

"Hot pepper? What do you mean?"

"Like a jalapeno?" Ron asked.

Anna just quickly nodded her head.

"How the heck would that get into your water bottle?" I asked. "Oh no, Ron, do you meditate with your eyes closed?"

"Always."

"Did you notice anything?" I asked.

"Just my breathing."

"For how long?"

"I was focusing on the present," he said.

"Sorry?" I asked, thinking I hadn't heard him right.

"There is only 'clock time in the now'."

"Yeah, and she's running out of it," I told him. "Anna, how long were you in the bathroom?"

Her eyes were watery and bloodshot. She could only speak between rough, guttural coughs. "I don't know, twenty minutes?" She shook the empty bottle. "Need more."

"Anna Swenson, you're up," said the casting assistant.

"You're gonna be fine," I said, as convincingly as I could, while black mascara dripped down her face.

I ran up to the stage door. "Hi, we're having a bit of problem."

"Are you Anna?" the assistant asked.

"No, I'm trying out for Rizzo, but you see, my friend, well …"

"You're not on for a while."

"That's fine, but my friend's voice seems to have disappeared momentarily."

"Well, we took all the Sandys first. I can talk to the director, but she's our last one. The Dannys are next. Maybe we can fit her in later on. I'll ask, okay? But for right now, we have to keep going." The assistant glanced down at her clipboard. "Okay, can all the Dannys listen up? We're moving on to you guys, so let me have Matt Barkley."

Matt came down the other side of the hallway with Cindy holding onto him like he was her academy award nominated man walking the red carpet. I had a feeling their breakup wasn't going to last. What he sees in her is a complete mystery.

"Oh, hey, Casey," Matt said, "you here with Anna?" The adrenaline of the audition put Matt's mouth on autopilot. As Anna's name slipped out, I could feel Cindy's hands tighten around his bicep.

"Yes, yes, I am. Her audition went great. I'm thinking she'll definitely get the part."

"Wait, she already auditioned?" Cindy asked, while peeking down the hall at Anna, who was busy coughing up her second lung. People were moving away from her, like she had some contagious pathogen, and yes, another irony. Anna was the last person people should have been afraid of. Ron stood loyally by her side, looking concerned, but helpless. Cindy didn't seem convinced. "Sounds like she could use more water," Cindy said, a creepy expression on her face.

"Matt Barkley, you're on," said the assistant with the clipboard.

Matt looked extremely relieved to exit this conversation as he released his arm from Cindy's vise.

"Okay then. Gotta go."

Cindy grabbed his face and gave him a big kiss on the mouth. "Break a leg, babe."

Considering the source, that statement did not ring true as a cheer of support but rather a threat of physical harm if Matt happened to look in the direction of another girl. I had to get away from her before I completely erupted.

"If Anna's throat clears and she does end up auditioning …" Cindy said as I walked away.

"She already did."

"But when she really does, if she does, let her know that I've plenty more water for that cotton mouth of hers, or whenever she requires it."

I looked straight at her and could have sworn there were black bats fluttering inside her eyes instead of pupils. "Then I'll have a little something for you as well. Just to show our appreciation for all you've done." I started to walk away only to turn back around to see her catching flies with her mouth. "See you at opening night. I'm certain Matt and Anna will give us a great show. Ta-ta."

After three more bottles of water and almost a pint of vanilla ice cream, the fire in Anna's throat was beginning to cool. They had just announced the Rizzo auditions and I knew I would be going in soon.

"How are you feeling?" I asked her.

"Like there is a load of cement solidifying in my stomach. Other than that, my throat hasn't completely melted," she said with a tired smile.

She was handling this much better than me and really deserved a chance at the part.

"After my tryout, I'm going to explain the situation again to the director. I can't imagine they won't let you audition."

"Thanks, Casey, but maybe it just isn't meant to be. I'm actually feeling pretty sick to my stomach."

"That's just nerves."

"And too much ice cream and a gallon of water."

"You'll be two-hundred percent when you get up there on stage."

The casting director called out, "Casey Riley, you're up."

"Be brilliant, girlfriend," Anna said with a smile.

Wow, here she was, dealing with the death of her dad just six months ago, and now this. And still, she was thinking about me now and not whining about her own bad luck.

"Yeah, just like you'll be on opening night."

I headed over to the stage door and out walked Sylvia Buchwald, looking calm, poised and pretty.

"Oh, hey, Case," she said.

I hated it when she referred to me with the one-syllable version of my name: that was only reserved for my family. Carly never even called me 'Case.' She didn't need to. It came off as a fake way to lighten things up and Sylvia was pretty damn plastic. Carly always said that Sylvia gave her the chills, but understood why I had to make nice. It was more out of an obligation to my sister Patty, who was gaga over the older brother, Brad. That was, before he broke her heart.

They had dated in high school and were considered the dream-teen couple of the community. Both were on our high school swim team, and Brad made all state, whereas my sister merely made all county, in the 50-meter swim competition. Brad ended up getting into Princeton on a swim scholarship, and Patty didn't. And here is another one of life's frustrating ironies. Patty had the brains, but not the money. Brad had the money and the athleticism, but not the brains. He was an okay student, but Patty was the one who wrote the essay for his college application, as well as tutored him in all his classes. When she was up late at night burning the midnight oil, she wasn't doing her homework. She was doing his.

After Patty got admitted to Princeton, she was the happiest I had seen her in a long time. She always struggled with her self-esteem, and in a rich town like Riverton, where everyone seemed to go on nicer vacations, drive nicer cars, and have nicer homes, her low level of confidence, and living in the smallest house on the block, took a toll.

Being with Brad helped build her up somewhat, but getting into Princeton on her own merit, that made her soar.

Patty came into our living room and laid the bittersweet bombshell on my parents' lap. My father's advertising agency had just lost two major accounts due to the 2008 bankruptcies of those 'we know better than you' financial firms. As a result, my mother's real estate business was seeing more short sales than sales. There was no way my folks could afford Princeton, unless of course, they were handed a bailout. Nah, not gonna happen. My parents, like all hard-working, honest taxpayers, weren't 'too big to fail', and had to pay for the financial shenanigans of those privileged captains of profit who were above the law.

Irony strikes again.

"What are you saying? Are you saying I can't go to Princeton?" my sister asked, as the snot ran down her nose and her eyes swelled up with tears.

"No, honey, we're not saying that. What we're saying is that right now we can't foot the bill for the entire amount. Perhaps you can apply for an academic scholarship," said my dad.

"Dad, my grades are good, good enough to get in, but those few kids who are getting merit scholarships scored a perfect 1600 on the SATS. The competition to get into Princeton is fierce and I did it. But the competition to have it paid for is impossible."

"Then wait a year or two. Work for a while, save up some money, and by then our situation will probably have gotten better. And work experience before college would offer you an advantageous perspective that you wouldn't have otherwise."

"Wait a year or two? 'Advantageous perspective.' My God, are you kidding? Brad will have probably moved on by then with someone else."

"Good," I said. "If he doesn't think you're worth waiting for, then he isn't worth running after."

All three turned to look at me like I had just woken up from the dead. I had, until now, remained pretty silent about

Brad. Patty thought I was friends with Brad's sister and wanted to remain neutral on their relationship, but the truth was, I didn't like him.

In fact, I just realized at this moment, I never really liked Sylvia.

It was now pretty clear to me that we only started hanging out in the first place because of Brad and Patty. This became more obvious when my sister got a full academic scholarship to one of the best state schools in New York. She ended up going that fall, and after her first year had already made Dean's List and was the editor of her school paper, unheard of for a freshman. And she did that while healing a broken heart from being dumped by the Bradster.

I wasn't surprised that after he broke it off with Patty, Sylvia came up with more and more reasons why she and I couldn't get together. We'd make plans to meet and she would show up almost an hour late. As if it was okay to leave me hanging. Like, who was I? Just the sister of the sister whose brother dumped her because her parents couldn't afford sending her to the same "icy" league school as him.

"Hey, Sylvia," I said, as I walked right past her onto the stage.

"You here to audition?" she asked, as if that was the most unlikely of events. She knew I could sing, so the question was odd. Then again, she was odd.

"Nah," I said. "Stage needs sanding."

I found out on Monday that I got the part of Rizzo. I also got a text from Ron that he couldn't wait to start rehearsals with me next Saturday. Anna, unfortunately, never even tried out. She was just too sick to make it happen, which was so wrong.

She deserved, and needed, to be involved with something she loved to do this summer. Losing her dad, and moving away from all her friends in the city, was just too much. Her mood went into a tailspin, and that just wasn't like her. Cindy Bender needed to know what she did would not go unnoticed. She had to be stopped.

Matt did get the part of Danny. This other girl from the next town up, who was dating an army ranger just back from serving one tour in Afghanistan and another in Iraq, landed the role of Sandy. I thought that would be a safe duo for Cindy to deal with. If the guy could survive a recurring shower of rockets and gunfire while living outside in the frigid mountain air, only to be dropped in a boiling sandbox lined with IEDs, he could handle Cindy. But my wheels were spinning and I just couldn't let this go. I had to send a message that her actions had consequences, so I started to think, and that is never good.

R on was a huge animal lover and for the past several summers had worked at an animal shelter near his grandfather's farm in North Carolina. He walked, fed, comforted and cleaned up after dogs that were abandoned or mistreated. During the year, he organized a foster program up at his private school to take in lost dogs and get students to look after them until he could find good homes. Animals technically weren't allowed in the dorms, but he sold his idea to the administration as good PR for the school, promoting responsibility. Parents ate it up. Score another huge eight, nine and ten points of attraction for Ron. As shelters go, the one in Riverton was not bad. Ron told me he had seen far worse when he worked down near Asheville. He spared me the ugly and sad details.

The Riverton shelter seemed to be where every lost animal, bird, rodent and reptile ended up. It had been a couple of years since I had been there. I used to go over with my mom, who volunteered walking the dogs. That was before she got entrenched in her real estate wars. Ron told me the staff had thinned out quite a bit over the last year or so and more volunteers were used to provide care and comfort. The financial crash didn't just affect people. The town had slashed the operating budget for the shelter, so the animals were feeling the brunt of it. Two weeks ago, when Ron showed up for a summer job, he discovered most fulltime staffers were fired. He was eighteen and took on the responsibilities of the onsite kennel manager, with offsite supervision from an overpaid, underworked, apathetic animal-control director located ten miles away. "Use your passion, son. You'll do fine," was about all he said, after he shook Ron's hand and jumped in his Lexus and drove away. Rumor had it that the shelter was going to close over the next few months anyway, unless someone stepped in to save it. "Animal Control" would most likely mean animal elimination. Though I was having a tough time believing that horrible prediction.

As I said before, I love all creatures great and small, both cold and warm blooded. Looking back on what I did, I realize now that the judge was right. My actions could have proved dangerous.

That is, dangerous to the poor king snake when I put him in the way of Cindy's toxic path.

If you want a pet snake, a king snake is the one to choose. They can grow to almost seven feet long, but are relatively docile, definitely non-venomous, and immune to the poison from other snakes. They are also constrictors and strangle their prey, such as a rattlesnake or a cottonmouth, then swallow them whole. Which is why you should never hurt a king snake. It's a good snake that helps get rid of the dangerous ones. So when Ron told me about George, the neighborhood king snake sunning himself behind a lawn chair outside the shelter, I knew he would be the perfect teacher for someone like Queen Cindy. Okay, I didn't intend to have her strangled and eaten whole, but I did like the metaphor.

George was about as long as an eastern king snake can grow. He was also beautiful with black and white stripes. Ron said that some snakes, king snakes in particular, start out as pets only to escape somehow, or get released, because the owners have grown bored with the responsibility and expense of feeding them mice, rats or whatever. During the day, George slithered around and got rid of those pesky, rather large, rats that loved to scurry around because of all the garbage and feed.

Wednesday, after school, Ron had asked if I wouldn't mind manning the phones for two hours. They had just lost their receptionist, so I was happy to help out. When I went through the rear entrance, I had to step over George, stretched out on the patio where the sun hit it just right, relaxing in the warmth. He had his own large, comfortable aquarium that he slept in at night when the shelter closed for the evening. I thought that would be the best time to make my move.

I had a few logistical challenges that needed to be worked out. One was, how the heck was I going to get him from here to wherever I was going to take him? I didn't even drive. Well, correction, I did drive, I just didn't drive legally. I possessed a learning permit and had been driving a stick shift, no less, for the past few months. Granted, I had never ventured beyond the parking lot of the multiplex cinema where my sister would take me early in the morning. But my acceleration was smooth, and my stops even smoother. I was a natural. When I took my test in a few months, Patty said I would definitely pass.

That was before my conviction.

My parents were away enjoying a bit of alone time up in Saratoga Springs. I was happy they had taken a college friend's offer of a reunion up by his lake-front home. My father had finally secured a few high-profile accounts and my mother's real estate business was becoming a bit more active. They had both worked really hard to get through and deserved to bask in the sun, and celebrate a little bit of long overdue profits. Not to mention it gave me a golden opportunity to borrow the car. I would just have to wait until my sister, home for the summer, went out with friends, which usually happened around 6:00. I was expected at the theater at 7:30, and since the shelter also closed at 6:00, I had some time to work with. I knew Cindy's MO. She would also be there with Matt, sitting in the seats, swooning over his every note, thinking each one was meant for her, while watching him closely next to his beloved Sandy.

It was still light outside, so before heading out of the garage, I put on my dad's large fishing cap and sunglasses, in the hope that the neighbors' prying eyes couldn't see it was little old me driving our Subaru hatchback. Fortunately, the shelter was just a five-minute drive from my house and the theater was down the street from the shelter. It was now 6:30. By this time, it would be closed and I should be alone.

I remembered there was a window in the back by the garbage cans that had a broken latch. It was easy to pry it open with a stick. I lifted myself up onto the garbage cans and climbed through. I made my way down the hall and into the windowless back room where George was curled up like a wound-up garden hose. I went into the storage area and saw his smaller carrying cage and a pushcart. I put the carrier on the cart and rolled it over to his aquarium. I opened both latches and was about to lure him into the transport case with a chicken egg when the beam from a bright flashlight caught me in mid motion.

"What are you doing here?" said a familiar voice. I could make out the outline of someone, who became quite clear to me when he flicked on the overhead lights.

"What are you doing here?" I asked. "Shouldn't you be at the theater?"

"I work here," Ron said. "Shouldn't you be at the theater?"

I looked at my watch. "Nah, I'm good. I have an hour to spare, and besides, George was looking a little thin the other day."

"Casey, seriously. You broke in. That is not good."

"No, what's not good is a window with a broken latch, where anyone could enter with far more evil intentions than the feeding of a king snake."

"What are you doing with George?" he asked.

"I have an egg in my hand. What does it look like I'm doing?"

"And with the other hand, you're opening the door to his transport cage. Where are you taking him?"

And with that, George started slithering out of his aquarium and into the carrying case, where I placed the egg.

"To the theater. I thought he could use a night out."

"Look, I don't have much time. You want to tell me why you're stealing George?"

"I'm not stealing George. I'm just borrowing him to teach that poisonous asp, better known as Cindy Bender, a lesson."

Ron sat down on the chair, swiping his long blond bangs out of his eyes. He was actually quite cute when he got serious.

"I can't let you do that," he said.

"Just go away. You were never here. In fact, I don't even see you now. You're a dream."

*"I'm a dream?"*

"A figment of my imagination."

"Okay, listen. I know Cindy did a bad thing, but ..."

"No, you listen. She has been bullying kids for years now. She did it in elementary and now this. She hurt Anna, Ron. I don't mean just freaked her out, but charred her vocal cords so she couldn't even speak, let alone hit a high note. Cindy sabotaged Anna's audition, completely ruining her summer.

After what that poor girl has been through, that is so wrong. It will just continue and continue, until Cindy knows what it's like to have it thrown right back at her. No one seems to get that she has no fear of authority. King George is what she will understand. Pure and simple."

"What were you planning on doing?"

"I thought you'd never ask."

"Not now. I have to get over to the theater."

"Great, I'll explain while we go over there. But can we just take George? Oh, and could you follow me to my house? I have to drop off my car."

"Is that your car out front? You're not old enough to drive."

"I was born to drive."

I pulled into my garage without incident. No police cars were waiting in my driveway, and my sister was still out with friends. I jumped into Ron's pickup, where George was safely secured inside his plastic aquarium in the back.

"You know, I could lose my job over this."

"Then who'd run the place? No one is going to take a job that lasts two months until the place closes down."

"That's just a rumor."

"I certainly hope so."

"It doesn't matter. I saw what happened to Anna, and you're right, it was messed up. But I'm not letting you have George until you tell me what you're planning."

I was actually still working out the kinks. Ron was waiting for my response, and then flashed me a crooked smile that made my stomach jump a few flights.

"You have no idea, do you?" he asked.

"I thought it would become clearer once I had George in my possession."

"Then let's forget it for now. We gotta go anyway. I'm dropping George back off at the shelter and you and I can hash this out later."

"No, wait." I put my hand on his arm. "You and I aren't even rehearsing together tonight. I'm with the rest of the girls in an hour, and you're with Danny and Sandy now. I'll wait in the parking lot with George until you're done, then you hang out and wait for me. Deal? By then, I'll have a plan."

Ron shook his head, as if to say, *why am I even considering this?* and then flashed me another one of those smiles. He headed down the road toward the theater, then parked towards the back of the lot and turned off the ignition.

"All right. If you get bored, there are a few books under the seat. Help yourself."

"Okay."

I watched him walk inside the theater and realized he was right. He had a pretty cool summer gig going and I didn't want to jeopardize that. But there was no way anyone could trace George to the shelter. King snakes were native to the area and George might easily be wild. I turned around and saw that he was just chilling out, coiled around leaves and cedar chips. I reached in the back and picked up *Chains* by Laurie Halse Anderson. This was actually one of my favorite books that Mr. D had recommended. I loved stories about real events that happened in the past. It was a pain-free way of learning without having to study. This was about a young slave girl during the American Revolution. She was asked to spy for us while we were fighting for our own freedom from the Brits, yet we wouldn't give her the right to freedom. Talk about irony.

Forty minutes passed, and I was really getting into the story again when I was interrupted by yelling out in the parking lot. I looked up, and then quickly ducked down lower in the seat. Matt was running after Cindy, who was flailing her arms like someone directing traffic in the middle of a busy intersection.

"I can't trust you for a minute, can I?" she yelled.

"We're just rehearsing. It's a play. I'm supposed to be hot for Sandy. How can I show that without touching her?"

"Touch her? You were all over her."

Matt tried to grab Cindy's arm and she pushed him so hard that he almost tripped and fell to the ground. Then Sally Peck's BMW flew into the driveway and skidded to a stop. The back door flew open and Cindy jumped in. The car sped off, leaving Matt in a cloud of dust. He just stood, looking off in the car's direction, then turned back toward the theater, shaking his head as he went. I knew where Cindy was heading in order to commiserate with her buddies over pizza and Diet Coke ice cream floats. That was another one of her MOs. I had seen and heard it before: in the cafeteria, in the quad outside the smoking area, in the parking lot waiting for the bus. Cindy was one drama queen, and had an entourage of subjects who served her, which still baffled me.

When Ron walked out with Matt, it didn't take long for him to jump in his car to take off. I decided to text the director and made an excuse to miss my first rehearsal.

> So sorry, bad pizza for lunch, should be fine for tomorrow.

"You sure you want to do that?" Ron asked, as he slid into the driver's seat.

"This is more important. Besides, first rehearsals are just read-throughs anyway."

"Not for Danny. He was playing his part all out with Sandy."

"Yeah and I heard Cindy didn't take it too well."

"I'm beginning to see she doesn't take anything too well."

Ron started his car and we drove over to the lot at *Sal's Pizzeria* and parked in the back.

"Now what?"

"Just wait," I said.

We saw Matt's car pull in, his brakes screeching to a quick stop.

"It all depends on whether they are making up, or breaking up," I added.

We watched Matt fly out of his car and enter Sal's. Through the large window we could see Cindy sitting at a booth with three members of her goon squad. Matt approached calmly and tried to sit down, but Cindy blocked him with her hands, like one of the Supremes singing *Stop in the Name of Love*. Sally Peck placed her hand on Cindy's shoulder to bring her back down to earth.

"Uh-oh, not a good move, Sally," I said.

Then Cindy pushed Sally's hand away, rose up out of the booth and flew out the door, followed by Matt.

"Duck," Ron said, as the two of us dropped down in our seats. Our heads came comfortably close. "Definitely a break-up," he said.

"Or, she's playing self-entitled queen-o-rama, which is pretty much what she does."

"Yeah, like all girls," he said. I gave him a look. "Well, maybe not all."

I peeked out the window and saw Cindy running down the parking lot away from Matt's car.

"Let's move." I jumped out and grabbed George's cage. Ron quickly helped me carry it over to Matt's car. We opened up the back door and gently placed George onto Matt's back seat.

"Oh, man. How are we going to get George back?"

"We'll appear out of nowhere, like celebrity snake whisperers."

"What? Like Steve Irwin."

"Exactly."

"Remember what happened to him?"

"Stop worrying."

"And when are we going to make this appearance?"

"We'll hear her."

"Hear her?"

"Screaming."

"How do you know they'll end up in the same car?"

"Because they're heading to Sunset Ridge?"

"How the heck do you know that?"

"Because that's where everyone goes to make up and make out."

"And how do you know that?" Ron asked, while showing me those dimples of his again.

"If you went to school here, you'd know that. Besides, I do have an older sister."

"I know one thing. If I were Matt, I'd let her go. There is way too much going on in that head of hers," Ron said.

"Kind of frightening,"

Their argument had quieted down, so I looked up and could see the two crazies hugging. "Okay then, she's going with him. Let's get in your car and wait."

"What if George starts slithering toward them while they're driving?"

"Isn't he usually quiet for a bit while he's digesting?"

"Yeah, after he's swallowed a rabbit, but not a chicken egg."

"Frankfurter."

"What?"

"I gave him a frankfurter."

"Oh, God, watch him get car sick."

We squatted down behind other parked cars and made our way over to Ron's pickup. Soon Cindy and Matt headed over to his truck and got in. The lights from Sal's lit the car window perfectly and we could clearly see they were making up.

"Oh, come on. Make your move," Ron said.

"He's digesting. Give him time," I said.

"I'd rather George got friendly with her now than out on the open road."

And just then, Matt started up his car and headed out of the parking lot.

"Oh, no, go, go, go," I said.

"Oh, God, I'm going," Ron said.

We followed Matt out of the lot and onto the street.

"Oh, God," Ron said.

"Stop saying that. You're making me nervous."

"Well, I am nervous."

The drive up to Sunset Ridge wasn't far, but it was all uphill with a lot of hairpin turns. We were right behind them when Matt stopped at a light. Through their rear window, we could make out the silhouette of George's body slithering up toward the passenger seat.

"This is not good," Ron said.

Matt made a hard left at the sign for 'Sunset Ridge.'

"No, this is good. The dirt road up to the ridge is empty. Nothing bad is going to happen." I was totally lying.

Just then a car coming down the canyon road beamed his lights into Matt's window and we could see Cindy jumping around in her seat, like she had dropped a hot drink in her lap.

Suddenly, Matt slowed down, his door flew open, and he jumped out. The oncoming car had to swerve out of his way, barely missing him, and veered off the road into a small gully.

"There's no one driving Matt's car!" Ron screamed.

"Why the heck didn't he just throw it in park?" I asked.

"Because George is probably wrapped around the gear shift. How is that other car that just passed us?"

I turned around and noticed three passengers beginning to get out of the car, looking dazed, but unharmed.

"They're just in a little ditch. They're okay. Okay?" I said, not believing a word of it. In truth, I was freaking out as well.

Then the passenger door of Matt's car flew open. Cindy surprised me with an impressive stunt move, jumping out of out of the slow coasting car and rolling to the side of the road. Ron swerved around her as she looked up and saw me through the window, with an expression on her face that both pleased and gave me the chills. We drove on up ahead and parked behind a group of large boulders. As we got out, we heard a loud cracking sound as Matt's car broke through the low-lying bushes that lined the dirt road and finally came to a clunky stop.

"I gotta get George," I said as I ran over to Matt's car. When I got there, the passenger door was open and the snake nowhere inside.

"Oh, God," Ron said as he ran up to Matt's car.

"If you say that one more time, you'll be introduced. Come on, George is around here some place."

"George," Ron said quietly as he searched through the brush. "Come on, buddy."

"Do you have a flashlight?" I asked.

"Yeah, in my glove compartment."

I went back to Ron's truck to get the flashlight, and grab another treat out of my bag. I ran back and handed him the light. He waved the beam around the tires then shined it on a soft mound of moss where George was coiled around a log, partially hidden by a bushy pine branch. I bent down and tried to lure him out with another foot-long.

"I don't think he's hungry," I said.

"Can you blame him?"

"All right, just help me carry him back up to your car."

The two of us grabbed opposite ends and started back to the car, when a flashlight beamed in our faces.

"What did I tell you, Matt," said Cindy, with her hands on her hip. "And you thought she was so nice."

"Yeah, just like you're nice, right, Cindy?" I said.

Cindy had sticks coming out of her hair and Matt looked a little muddy, but other than that, they were in okay shape.

"Is that snake yours?" Matt asked

"Actually, we found him on the side of the road. Here, Cindy, want to hold him?" I asked as I brought George closer.

"If you know what's good for you, you'll get that snake away from me," she hissed.

"Don't worry, he just eats rats and other venomous snakes, great for getting rid of cottonmouths."

"Cottonmouths? I didn't think we had any poisonous snakes around here." Matt said.

"Oh, they're closer than you think, right, Cindy? You know all about cottonmouths, don't you?" I asked

"I know you put that snake in our car."

"Speaking of cars," Matt said, scratching his head and pulling a leaf out of his hair, "where is mine?"

"I think it's just down the little incline by that pine tree," said Ron, still holding George, now wrapped around his arm.

"Oh, hey, Ron, good rehearsal tonight," Matt said, as if he just noticed Ron standing there helping me hold a six-foot king snake.

"It was. Should be a good show. You all right?"

"Yeah, I, uh, just want to try and start my car," Matt said, as he sleep-walked down the hill, shaking the cobwebs out of his head.

"Come on, Casey, let's get George home." We walked over to the car with Cindy following behind.

"So he is yours?"

"No, he belongs to the shelter," I said as Ron and I placed him in his cage. "And if you don't quit your crap, the next one I introduce you to won't be harmless."

"Uh, oh," Ron said, as the flashing light of a patrol car came up the road and parked right next to us. A police officer came slowly out of the car.

"You kids okay?" he asked.

"No, Officer, I'm not," said Cindy. "This girl," pointing to me, "has been stalking me for months and almost got my boyfriend and me killed when she put a ten-foot cobra in the back of his car."

"Me stalking you? Really?" *Pot meet kettle.* "I don't even want to be near you. And it's not a cobra, it's a harmless king snake, six feet, not ten," I said.

"All right," said the officer. "Where's this snake?"

"Right here, Officer." Ron directed the officer to the back of the car and pointed to the cage, where George was now safely resting.

"Wow," said the officer. "That's a big one. Where'd it come from?"

"From her," said Cindy, pointing her skinny, long-nailed finger at me.

"And which car was it in?" asked the officer.

At that point, Matt pulled up, driving his car. It had a few branches stuck in the bumper, but was otherwise undamaged.

"Howdy, Officer," said Matt.

"You all right, son?"

"We're good," said Matt, talking out the window. "No harm done."

"No harm done?" said Cindy. "I want this girl arrested."

"Cindy, get in the car," Matt said.

"So, let me get this straight," the officer asked Cindy. "You believe this girl," meaning me, "put this snake in your car? For what purpose?"

"To warn her she can't continue to sabotage people's lives, or abuse them because she's jealous, or angry, or they have something she doesn't," I explained.

"So, you did put this snake in her car?" the officer asked.

"Actually, Officer, it's my car, and really, the snake just scared us. It didn't do any damage," Matt explained.

"What are you doing, Matt? Why are you giving her an out? This could have been serious."

"Like what you did to Anna wasn't?" I asked.

"I didn't try to kill her."

"Ah, so you admit it," I said.

Matt's face fell when he looked at Cindy. "You had something to do with that?" I was surprised he knew so little about the girl he'd been dating. He sounded really pissed. Cindy could sense that and was beginning to lose her cool, tough demeanor.

"It was just a little hot jalapeno sauce. I didn't think she would overreact the way she did."

I couldn't believe what I was hearing. "Overreact? Are you kidding me? You freak out over a hangnail, Cindy. What you did to Anna was cruel and painful, and you have the nerve to say she overreacted."

"You sabotaged her audition, why?" Matt's voice grew louder with every word. "Why would you do that? What were you thinking?"

I thought Cindy was going to cry, so I decided to go in for the kill. "Because she's jealous of anyone who has something she doesn't—beauty, inside and out, brains and talent. And that involves you, Matt. Though from the expression on your face that might be coming to an end real quick." *Gee, that wasn't very nice. Oh well.*

I felt I was winning this little war until the officer turned his attention on me. "In the juvenile court, all that would be considered irrelevant, young lady. But your actions here tonight wouldn't be. This could have caused a bad accident. You all are lucky," the officer said. "I'm afraid you'll have to come with me to the police station and call your parents."

"My parents are away on a trip."

"How nice for them, and how convenient for you," Cindy said.

I kept my mouth shut this time. Cindy had no clue about my parents, how hard they worked, and that it had been years since they'd had a break. If I spoke, bullets would have fired out of my mouth, which wouldn't have helped my cause down at the police station.

"My parents will be back in a few days. I'd hate to bother them. It's been a long time since they've been able to get away."

"Oh, brother, where are the violins? You should have thought about that before you tried to kill us."

"Shut up, Cindy," Matt said loudly. I had never heard him talk like that. I think Cindy was even surprised. I thought I was seeing things, but her eyes started filling up with tears. She noticed me staring and turned quickly around.

"My sister is home. She's twenty-one," I lied. "You can call her." Patty was actually only twenty. Nervousness always made my mouth go into overdrive. But after what I had just done, taking one year off Patty's life was the least of my concerns.

"We'll do that. But I'm afraid this is serious enough that your parents will have to be notified soon."

"What about me?" Ron said. "Aren't I an accomplice?"

"I don't know, are you?" asked the officer.

"No, he isn't," I said. "What are you talking about, Ron? Officer, I asked for Ron's help to get George back. He had nothing to do with my stealing George from the shelter, or in planting him in Matt's car."

"Is George the snake?" the officer asked.

"Yes," Ron and I said simultaneously.

"Who let you into the shelter?"

"I—" Ron said.

"I broke in," I said, interrupting Ron.

"You broke in," the officer said.

"Casey, what are you doing...?" Ron said.

"Ron, you should get George back. I'm really sorry for all this." There was no way I could involve him anymore and have him risk his job because of me.

"Okay, let's go, Officer."

I was escorted to the police car and got in the back. As we started to pull away, Ron shook his head. I thought he was angry at first. Then, I saw that grin of his, and when he waved goodbye, I knew he was more disappointed I got caught.

P atty showed up an hour after I got to the station. She was actually pretty cool. We both felt bad that we had to interrupt our parents' trip. That was the worst part about this whole thing.

The next morning, it didn't take long for my cell phone to buzz. It was a text from Ron.

How u doin?

> Not bad for someone facing charges of reckless endangerment and breaking and entering.

Can you talk?

> Now? Yes. Tomorrow? Unlikely.

Just then my phone rang. I answered it.

"Hey," Ron said.

"Hey. Looks as if I have to appear in front of the juvenile court."

"Ouch."

"I told you. If you'd said you were involved from the start, that would have been bad for you and the shelter."

"Why the shelter?"

"Because it's obvious they need you. You tried to get me to think it through. I wasn't listening. I was too set on getting back at Cindy."

"Do you have any other prior convictions?" he asked.

"Who do you think I am, Lindsay Lohan?"

"No, it's just that I know a kid at school who had to serve one hundred hours of community service for a first offense."

"What did he do?"

"Spray painted a huge rock on top of the cliff that overlooks our school."

"That's all he did?" I asked.

"It's what he wrote."

"And what was that?"

"'Al Qaeda rocks!'"

"Get out," I said. "Is he crazy?"

"No, just stupid."

"Well, it is free speech."

"Not up there, it isn't. And besides, he defaced public property in a public park."

"Well, I wish I could have defaced Cindy."

"You know, maybe she's got something going on that we're not aware of."

"More like going off. There's no excuse for her being cruel."

"I'm not excusing what she did. I'm just saying that usually people who are abusive have been abused themselves."

"Then pick on the people who abused you. Don't hurt someone who had nothing to do with it, and especially a person as nice as Anna."

"Look, if the judge does order community service, it would make sense that it's at the shelter. I know they've had a lot of people in the past serve time there, and they do need the help."

"Cool." I responded, a little too quickly and enthusiastically, but I didn't care. Ron must have known being around him and the animals would make a fun time out of a bad situation.

"It could be a lot of hours in a short amount of time."

"So?"

"It could conflict with the play."

"Not cool."

The next day, I was ordered before the court.

At 3:15 my parents picked me up in front of school. They came directly down from Saratoga Springs and didn't even have a chance to stop home first and change. My father was wearing his old Fordham sweatshirt and a pair of blue jeans. My mother was in a pair of shorts and a sweater. If it wasn't for the circumstances, they looked casual and relaxed. They were anything but.

I opened the back door and quietly slid in so as not to disturb the Kraken. My father pulled out of the parking lot and headed over to the town hall.

"I'm sorry. Mom, Dad, I'm really sorry."

They both looked at each other. My mom spoke first.

"Case, we know you are, and quite frankly, even though we're surprised and disappointed you behaved so irresponsibly, we are more relieved that no one got hurt."

"You've always had a temper and stood up for those who need help. You've been this way for as long as we can remember. But you need to learn how to work through the proper channels."

"Dad, I tried. No one would listen. Except now, and I'm the one who has to face the consequences, not her."

"What you did was wrong, Casey. And it could have been really dangerous. Let's just be happy it turned out the way it did," my mom said.

"Except, Anna and I are the ones whose summer got ruined because of Cindy Bender."

"You don't know that yet. Perhaps you'll learn something about yourself after all this. Stranger things have happened." My dad parked and the three of us headed inside, down the long corridor to the courtroom. We sat and waited for the bailiff to call my name. I looked up at the bench, where Judge Centinio was seated. He wore a very serious expression, with a sharp, chiseled chin that didn't seem to move, except upward. Then a lawyer walked to the bench and said something that made him crack a smile. Okay, he was human. I would be okay. But as soon as the bailiff called my name, it was back to being stiff-chinned Centinio.

"Casey Riley, would you stand please?"

I thought they were calling someone else's name until my mother nudged my leg with her hand. I stood.

"Ah, yes, present."

"Would you state your name before the court?" the bailiff asked.

"Casey Riley, uh, Ms. Casey Riley. Casey. You can call me Casey."

Then the judge spoke with a voice like the wizard in *The Wizard of Oz*. A low sonic boom reverberated through the entire courtroom, making me want to duck and cover under the long table. I thought I would pass out.

"Casey Riley, you are here before the court today, June 19th, 2010 to face charges of reckless endangerment to five persons, namely: Cindy Bender, Matt Barkley, Tony and Dana Wright, and Tim Canton."

Five people? Oh, right. The other three people in the car that had to swerve out of Matt's way.

"How do you plead?" the judge asked.

"Guilty, your Honor. But there were reasons for my actions, sir. You see—"

Then the sound of the gavel hitting the bench ricocheted through the room, clamping my mouth shut.

"Are Mr. and Mrs. Riley here today?" the judge asked.

"Yes, your Honor," my father said, taking my mother's hand as they both stood up next to me.

"Miss Riley," the judge said, "I'm certain your parents explained how serious the results of your actions could have been."

"Yes, sir, they did."

"You are very lucky no one sustained any serious injuries."

"Well, that's not entirely true, your Honor." My mother's foot hit my shin.

"Oh?" the judge asked. "This is new information I was not aware of." He looked to one of the lawyers. "Mr. Jenson, do you have any updates you would like to add?"

"No, your Honor, I'm unaware of any physical injuries sustained as a result of Miss Riley's actions."

"That's because they happened before this incident. I did what I did to stop Cindy Bender from hurting anyone else. Talk about '*breaking and entering.*' She broke into my friend's locker and damaged her property. She also '*endangered*' her by burning out her throat with some jalapeno witch's brew before she was supposed to audition for the summer production of *Grease*, thereby ruining her summer and the ability to get over her father's death. And these incidents are just in the last few months on the one person I happen to know personally. The Bender terror has been reigning in Riverton for years now. I felt it was my duty as a citizen of this town, and as a student at George Washington High, to try and prevent anyone else from getting hurt. Oh, and by the way, there is a window lock in the back of the shelter that needs repairing before anyone else breaks in, your Honor, which they really don't have to do, because it's already broken."

I looked over at my father, who had a slight grin on his face. My mother on the other hand looked as if she overdid the Botox. Her eyes were wide open and locked at an unnatural height.

The judge just stared down on me in silence. I felt like hours went by before he spoke.

"I understand, Miss Riley, that you felt you were acting in the community's best interest, but in point of fact, you weren't. Many people could have been seriously hurt. The accusations involving Cindy Bender's prior activity, though disturbing if accurate, are irrelevant to your case. You should have gone to the proper authorities regarding these incidents that you speak of."

"I did, your Honor," I said, right before my mother tugged hard on my braid.

"Nevertheless, these charges against you are not taken lightly in my court, and since you mentioned the condition of the shelter's building, and perhaps could use some increased understanding about an animal's or reptile's welfare, I sentence you to one hundred fifty hours of community service at the Riverton Animal Shelter, to be completed within the next two months, commencing this Friday, the 22nd of June."

I immediately started calculating how many hours a week that would be. Whew! Completely manageable to do while staying in the play. The flock of geese that had been flying around in my stomach finally landed.

The drive back to the house was not as eerily quiet as the drive over. My parents were talking about what fun they had until Mr. Fuller, that's my dad's old roommate from school, took them on a boat ride on his new Ferretti 200.

"He sure showed us who was Captain of that ship," my dad said. "It was 'watch out for this' or 'wouldn't do that' or 'can you help with this.' Wow, Fuller was quite full of himself."

My mom said Dad was exaggerating, and they had a great day aboard the new yacht, which my father said was smaller than Mr. Fuller's head. Still, Mom was not overly bummed about leaving a day or two early. She had landed a couple of new listings and was anxious to start showing them. I think they were also relieved I wasn't sentenced to anything more serious than community service at a nearby shelter. But then they dropped the bomb. Summer was going to be a busy time at my mom's office and she could really use the extra help, especially now that she was beginning to make a name for herself. My dad even tried to put a positive spin on it.

"Don't you want to start saving up for that car of yours?" he asked

"But how many hours are we talking here? Can I fit it in with being in the play while working in the shelter? I do have a major role."

My answer came when my mom's cell started ringing. She had just landed another listing on a million-dollar home up in the hills. She was beaming. My dad gave her a kiss on the cheek. Believe it or not, I was really happy for her, while at the same time I wanted to jump out of the car screaming that '*life wasn't fair!*'

R on said it, there was no way I could be in the musical now. That made two summers Bender had ruined, Anna's and mine. Who knew how many others there had been. Maybe my dad was right, some good could come out of all this. But right now, as I imagined the joy of belting out those notes to a theater full of people, with Ron grinning by my side, (his hand in mine) it was hard to imagine what that would be.

When I walked into my bedroom, my phone was doing a jig on my table. It was Anna.

"You're nuts, you know that," she said.

"At least I'm a nice nut."

"I don't think Cindy would say that."

"Well, Cindy isn't nice."

"So true," Anna said.

I knew Anna wasn't at school today, and she was trying to hide how down she was about rehearsals starting and not being in the play due to what we called the 'Saturday sabotage.'

"You feeling okay?" I asked.

"Yeah. I was just really looking forward to focusing on something other than crying all the time. Grief gets to be a real yawner after a while."

"Anna, it was your dad. It only happened a short while ago, and it was sudden. You don't get over something like that too quickly." If you ever really do.

"That's just it, the musical would've helped. I'm just trying to figure out why these bad things keep happening to me. Like I'm jinxed or something."

"No. You're just pretty, and smart and talented. Insecure people have a tough time with that."

"If that's true, then I'm the one having a tough time with that." I could tell she had to stop for a second and swallow a few tears. I wished there was something I could do for her. I decided to just keep my mouth shut for once and let her speak. "It's okay," she continued. "I should be working this summer anyway and not pretending to be a musical star. We could use the money. But I think my mom is more upset that I am. She called Principal Langdon and he said there was really nothing he could do without any proof, especially since it was something that happened off school grounds."

"Your submerged locker was on school grounds."

"But there were no witnesses."

"Langdon is a lazy loser and is probably counting his days to retirement. You know what? My dad said something that may turn out to be true. This summer is going to be a good one. I don't know how just yet, but it will."

"You're going to be pretty busy with the show."

"I'm not going to be in the show."

"What? Why not?"

"I was sentenced to one hundred and fifty hours of community service at the shelter. I can't fit it in along with helping my mom out."

"I'm sorry, Casey."

"Well, at least we can both be mad together."

"I'm tired of being mad."

"You're right. Hey, maybe Ron can get you some paid work at the shelter. I know they need the help. Wait, you like animals, right?"

There was a pause of silence on her end, and then I heard what I thought was a sad snicker. "We lost our lab six months before losing my dad. You're going to think I'm horrible, but I don't know what was worse. When Sedona's heart went out. I thought mine was going to blow as well. She had cancer."

"That's a beautiful name."

"She was beautiful, and had the color of a southwest canyon when the sunset hit it just right. Her coat was a warm red brown that I loved to brush and run my hands through. She always smelled so good."

"Man, Anna, you've had a tough year. Okay, time to change the frequency here. I'm going to talk to Ron and see what he can do. Would you like that?"

"I'd love it."

"Great, see you tomorrow? Only a few more days until summer."

"Yeah. See you at school."

"And I wouldn't worry too much about Cindy. I think my little stunt scared her off, at least for a while. She knows now I'm a rebel with a cause and she better stand down."

"Well, that makes two rebels."

"Good to know."

After I hung up with Anna, I lost track of how long I had been lying on my bed. I was thinking about how bummed I had been over giving up my summer, and dream part, while at the same time angry with myself for feeling that way. Talk about life not being fair. Anna was the one who had been through an emotional torture chamber and here I was whining. My mom knocked softly, then came in and lay on her side next to me.

"You okay?" she asked.

"I'm okay, Mom."

"Good. I know you know this, but it can never be said enough. Your father and I love you so much. And we are proud of you. I'm not happy with what you did, but I understand. Sometimes we feel our hands are tied, and we just need to break the cord any way we can to make a difference."

"I know, Mom. I was just thinking about how lucky I've been, and that maybe Dad was right. Maybe something good will come out of all this. It's kind of hard to see what that will be right now, but I'm going to look for it."

"Don't look too hard. You might plow right into it."

My mom came up with these life lesson statements that often didn't make any sense, until a few days, or weeks, or sometimes months later. "Meaning?"

"Maybe it's right in front of you. Don't go searching for it. You can't fix everything, okay? Just let it be."

"Okay," I said, while releasing the bad air from my lungs.

I think my mental fog over everything that happened these last few months was lifting and I actually began to understand. Then again, I didn't see anything wrong with trying to help out a friend, especially someone like Anna, who, other than me, didn't have any friends yet. Perhaps I got a little blind with my agenda of getting back at Cindy and I took things a little too far. Maybe things did have a way of working themselves out if I would just leave things alone.

"Okay, let's get out of here and get some food. I'm starving. The Fullers are vegetarians and rail thin. I think they survive off the air."

"The air and all that money."

"Well, you can never be too thin or too rich."

"We're rich, Mom." I hugged my mother tightly, so thankful I had her and Dad in my life."

T he last Friday of school came, and I did end up being late for signing in at the shelter. I was helping Mr. Davis carry a few of his books out to his car and, as usual, we started talking.

"Thanks for the help, Casey."

"No, Mr. D., thank you for what you've done for me these past two years. I don't know if my dream of being a writer will ever come true, but at least I have a dream now."

"It's a muscle. Just because it's summer doesn't mean you should stop using it. Keep a journal, write for the local paper, keep reading, and write not just what you know, but what's important to you, what you can see and taste and smell. Keep it simple, but don't just draw the outline. Fill it in. It has to be real for you so it can be real for us."

"Hmm? 'Keep it simple,' but 'fill it in?' I don't think I get that."

"You will."

"Well, I'm going to be pretty busy this summer with two jobs, but...."

"Then use that."

"Use what?"

"What you experience from those two jobs. People are fascinating. Situations are interesting, as long as you breathe life into them. Don't show off what you know. Show us how it makes you feel."

"My parents say I show how I feel a little too much. Kind of how I landed in juvenile court."

"Start putting it all down in words. Not just how, but why you did it."

"I think you might have something there."

"I think you do."

Mr. Davis powered down the window and started up the engine.

"You ever coming back down this way, Mr. D.?"

"Oh, sure. Sarah and I will close up the cabin in late September and be back around then. Give us a call."

"I will definitely do that."

"But don't come empty handed. I want to see what you've written."

"Will do."

He pulled out of the lot and headed down the road. It was then I discovered I had another dream, just in case my first one didn't work out. I wanted to be as good a teacher as Mr. D. Then again, that might be just as tough, if not tougher, than dream one.

I threw my backpack over my shoulder and sprinted over to the shelter.

It was 3:45 when I walked up to the new receptionist, whom I had never seen before. I had thought there was a hiring freeze at the town. Then again, maybe she was a volunteer who just needed to keep herself busy. She was a much older woman who, quite frankly, didn't look like she could walk herself, much less walk a dog. She had a warm smile though and long white hair that hit her waist. She was wearing jeans, Birkenstock sandals, and a long white T-shirt that had an assortment of stains and smudges in various colors.

"Hi, I'm Casey Riley. Sorry, I'm late."

"Late for what?" the receptionist asked.

"I'm here for the community service ordered by the court."

"Oh. Yes, you're the one who stole George." She had a low raspy voice that sounded as if she had smoked one too many cigarettes in her time.

"I know, I'm so, so sorry about that. How's he doing? I didn't mean to hurt him. I didn't hurt him, did I?"

"George? No, he's fine. My name is Maureen, Maureen Kelley. And don't worry about being late. We're just happy for the help. Sign in and I'll get Ron, the kennel manager, to show you around."

Being new, I guess the old gal didn't realize that I understood the place better than most. I didn't want to insult her so I just let it alone. Besides, as juvenile court sentences go, this was not going to be painful. I looked for a sign in sheet, but didn't see one.

"I'm sorry where do I…?"

Maureen smacked her hands on her hip. "What do you know? She did it again."

"Who did what again?" I asked.

"Tango."

And just then, the strongest, meanest-looking pit bull peeked her massive brick-like head out from underneath Maureen's desk.

"Tango," Maureen said, pointing to the beast. "She gets jealous whenever I focus on something other than her. Like paper work. She ends up eating whatever it is I'm working on."

"You do realize your focus is on me right now?"

Maureen let out a deep, but warm, laugh. "Hah! I think you're a little too big."

"You sure about that?" This was one huge dog, and even though I knew Pit Bulls got a bad, undeserved rap, this dog was like a canine python that could swallow me whole.

"You see, I was transferring the names of the volunteers and potential adoptions into our database and she grabbed the sign-in sheet off my desk when I wasn't looking. You bad girl." Maureen took the large head in her small arthritic hands and began to rub Tango's ears, which she clearly enjoyed by the groan of pleasure and her rear end moving like a windmill. "Say hi to Casey, Tango. Here, Casey, come around the desk and meet Tango."

"Oh, that's okay, there's plenty of time for that. I should start working anyway."

"This is part of your work," Maureen said. "Oh, that's right, you used to volunteer here."

"Yes, guess I've been demoted."

"Not at all. We need all hands on deck. You'll be able to get up close and personal with the animals more than before."

I knew from watching Cesar Milan that dogs sensed fear, the last thing I wanted to relay to 'queen of the kennel' here. I took off my possibly threatening baseball cap and laid my backpack on the front counter. I opened up the swinging doors, and before I was able to get down on all fours, Tango made a beeline for me, with her butt wagging and head flopping. She walked through the front of my legs, tossing me off balance, then circled around back and sat down right in front of me. I started scratching behind her ears and she lay down on her back exposing her pink belly.

"She wants you to rub her stomach," Maureen said.

I sat down and did just that. She was warm and smooth and began whining with fun and delight. She then jumped back up and stared straight into my eyes, assessing me, knowing full well I was friend and not foe. She proved this by giving me her paw.

"She wasn't here last week," I said.

"No, my daughter and I found her tied up to a fire hydrant outside the movie theater three nights ago. Apparently she had been there all day long. No one has claimed her yet, which is fine by us. We'll give it another few days and then she's mine."

"She's so sweet. Hard to believe someone would just leave her like that."

"And without any water in the heat of the day. We see it all the time," Maureen added.

"That's why this shelter needs to stay open," I said.

"We'll make it happen somehow," Maureen said.

"I see you've made friends with the mayor."

I turned around. Ron was holding two of the cutest, reddish-brown puppies I had ever laid eyes on. He placed them on the ground next to Tango. They jumped all over her, biting her ears, her tail, and all she did was lick them clean. They followed her back to her warm, fluffy bed underneath Maureen's desk and nestled between her head and two front paws.

"Oh, my gosh. Are they hers?" I asked.

"Afraid not," Ron said. "They were found in an abandoned house up on Crescent Drive. We don't know what happened to the mother. They were close to dead when we got the tip. A jogger running through the trail nearby heard them crying. Maureen's daughter and I went out there and found them in a hot closet with no water, no food, just lying there in their own pee and poop."

"Oh, God." I crawled over to Tango and was about to pick one of them up when Ron stopped me.

"Casey, I wouldn't do that." Ron said it calmly, but I could tell he was serious. I immediately pulled back.

"Tango probably wouldn't do anything, but she may sense that they've been through hell and back. She could be protective," he added.

"Well, I understand that. I'm known to be kind of protective myself." I sat down cross-legged next to the three dogs. "I get it, girl. You're a good girl." And with that, Tango looked at me with eyes that would melt a glacier, and rested her head on top of the sleeping puppies.

R_____ _____ _ helped me to my feet. "Well, I'd sa_____ laureen?"

'

' love conquered your fear. Tan

"Well, I wouldn't want to get on Tango's bad side."

"I don't think she has one, unless, of course, you mean to do her harm, which you don't," Maureen said.

"No, I sure don't."

Ron placed his hand on my shoulder "Come on, I want to show you a few of our new arrivals. Then you can come back and fill out some paper work."

"Sounds good."

"Take your time," Maureen said. "I'm usually here until past closing."

"Okay, thanks."

"No, Casey, thank you."

"Well, it wasn't really my doing."

"Yes, it was. If you hadn't kidnapped George to try and help a friend, you wouldn't be here now, able to help these animals. And let me tell you, they need it. Things do have a strange way of working out."

"Guess they do."

Ron took me through the glass doors of the lobby into the kennel area. Immediately an explosion of barking ricocheted through my eardrums. We passed by several kennels. Each one had a fluffy, warm-looking bed, blanket, large bowl filled with fresh water, and a few toys strewn around. Conditions had certainly improved over the last week.

"We've been trying to take the more difficult dogs out several times a day, which has been a little tough lately with the staff shortages. So as much as it's a bummer what happened to you, believe me, you are needed. It helps that we were able to fence in a large area in the back where we let most of the dogs out to run and play. We're in the process of fencing in another smaller yard for those individual cases. Unfortunately, not all dogs get along."

"Too bad Cindy can't be fenced in." Ron gave me a 'let it go' look and he was right. There was a reason I was here. "Well, not that this shelter was bad before, but I can see you've been busy and done a great job."

"I couldn't have done it alone. Maureen and her daughter Peggy have been here ten hours every day, as well as trying to negotiate a contract with the town."

"Does that mean you'll be able to hire more help?" I asked, for Anna's sake.

"We hope so. It's a political thing. I think I told you, the town board voted to close the shelter about six months ago. It's been tough going since the economy went into a tailspin. Funds have been slashed. They felt that the money going into feeding and taking care of abandoned or homeless animals was better spent fixing roads, playgrounds, football fields, and other necessities."

"Saving a life isn't a necessity?"

"Not when the life is an animal. I mean, I agree with you. Closing this shelter would have been a death sentence to many of them. The good news is some local residents fought the town, and the shelter has remained open. But it's running on a meager budget from just donations, with a staff filled mostly with volunteers. Fortunately, we have a lot of volunteers."

"I can't believe they were thinking of doing away with this shelter. The financial meltdown wasn't their fault."

"No argument from me," Ron said. "But it gets down to priorities. What's more important to some is last on the list for others. And now I see that a lot of things need to be repaired, supplies are low, and more important, some of these dogs need to be worked with."

"Worked with?" I asked.

"Well, some come from pretty tough backgrounds and are aggressive. They need to know they are safe, so they are safe to be around."

"I'll work with them."

"You're way too young."

"Says who?" I asked.

"According to the town, you have to be eighteen or older to do hands-on with the dogs. Of course, due to necessity, we can bend that rule a bit. The younger kids like you usually do the dirty work, you know, cleaning the kennels, or just walking them. Besides, we need professional trainers for rehabilitation and that costs money."

"Walking a dog is not dirty work," I said.

"Not for you, no, but for a lot of people it loses its charm real quick. It's one of the reasons why we have so many abandoned pets."

"So, can this group of local residents raise some money to help run the shelter better?"

"They are trying, and actually go one step further."

"What do you mean?"

"They're trying to make the shelter go private, take it out of the local government's hands. That way they don't have to wait for the town board to hold a vote for things like fixing the air conditioner when it's ninety-five degrees outside. It would be run by animal advocates who have only one agenda."

"Giving the animals a good home until they can find a better one."

"Yes. But again, it's all politics. Here, the town board was all in favor of letting the shelter go, but now that a private organization wants to come in and run it more efficiently, with one goal in mind, the mayor doesn't want to be shown up as incompetent, or worse, an animal hater."

"No, I wouldn't think voters like people who don't like animals."

"Exactly."

"So, what are you doing now about dogs that don't like people?" I asked.

"Well, those are challenges we've been trying to correct, but until we can hire trainers who have experience with these cases, it's tough. And you are about to meet one such challenge."

We stopped in front of the kennel that housed a large German shepherd-husky mix that could have jumped off the page from Jack London's *Call of the Wild*. And she did look wild, with a thick mane of silver fur that framed beautiful eyes the color of blue ice. As soon as we approached, she flew to the back of the cage and sat there shivering, like we were going to take her to the slaughterhouse. It broke my heart. I tried not to think about the circumstances that would make such a large, powerful, magnificent-looking animal so terrified.

Irony strikes again.

"Meet Sierra," Ron said. "It's okay, girl. Here, I've got something for you." Ron took out a plastic bag filled with slices of meat. "Here, beauty, I know you've got to like turkey." Ron placed a few pieces in a bowl hanging on the side of her kennel. Her body was stiff, except for her belly moving rapidly from heavy, anxious breathing. Eyes like crystals were locked on us like a laser, watching our every move. "It's hard," Ron said to me, "I don't want to cause her distress by trying to get closer, but at the same time, if I don't try, she'll never come out of this trauma."

I just wanted to nestle down next to her, but I think she would have squeezed through the wire to escape. She was petrified.

I was angry. "Who did this to her?"

"It's hard to tell. A guy brought her in last week."

"What guy?"

"It doesn't matter?"

"What do you mean, 'it doesn't matter?' He should be brought up on charges and thrown in a kennel half the size without food or water."

"He was dragging her in on a leash. She was trying to pull away from him and he just kept tugging her toward the shelter. I was here with one of the other volunteers and the dude said he found her on the side of the road and thought he should bring her here. Thing is, she has marks around her neck where the hair is worn away. Typical sign of being chained up for quite some time."

"Oh, God."

"I've seen this a lot. People get a dog and then underestimate the cost and time it takes to be a good owner. So they end up chained outside. They're vulnerable because they can't run away from whatever might be hurting them. At least the guy brought her in."

"So, you don't think he was just being a good Samaritan?"

"How could he? Sierra doesn't get close to anybody. You think some stranger is going to be able to put a collar around her and get her in their car? No, this story has been used too many times."

"I'll be able to get close to her, Ron. I will. I'll be patient. Please let me try. I mean, at least until you get someone else with more experience. What's the harm?"

"Casey, she's huge. She could be part wolf, for all I know. She could really hurt you. I don't know enough about her, nor do I have the experience."

"I'll stay outside the kennel."

Sierra was no longer sitting up, but crouched down in the corner with her head turned away from us. It was horrible to see her like this. I was caught between having to turn away, and again, wanting so badly to just prove to her right then and there that I would take care of her, and love her, for as long as her life allowed. But for right now, I couldn't do anything except stare at this poor animal with pity. I needed air and walked away. Ron followed me outside.

I stood looking off into the parking lot. I knew Ron was right behind me. "She won't hurt me. She's just scared."

"I know. Most aggressive dogs are scared. It's the fear of them being hurt that makes them lash out at anyone who threatens them."

"But Sierra isn't showing signs of aggression."

"Not yet. But she might if you get too close."

"I won't at first. I'm not stupid, Ron. I know I did a stupid thing with George and Cindy, and whatever, but I'll start out slowly. I'll just make friends with her outside the wire. See where it takes us."

"All right, but do not go inside. You promise?"

"What if it becomes obvious she trusts me?"

"Well, you can prove that to me, or the trainer, when we can hire one."

"So, you think it'll work. You believe she'll warm up to me?"

"I think it's possible, but only if you're patient."

"Patience is one of my strengths."

Ron shook his head, knowing full well I'd said the exact opposite just a few days ago.

"Okay, why don't you go and fill out that paperwork with Maureen and then I'll see you back here tomorrow at eight in the morning?"

"You got it." I started to walk away, and then, remembering Anna, I turned around to catch Ron before he headed back inside. "Hey, do you need any extra help?"

"What do you think?"

"Well, I know you do but, well, Anna lost her dad and dog about six months ago. I know she could use the distraction, and the money. I just don't know if the shelter can afford to pay her."

"Not yet, but if distraction is enough for now, like I said, we could use the help."

"I'll tell her."

"Okay, I gotta get those dogs outside in the yard to let off some steam. See you tomorrow."

I wanted to go back to the kennel area and hang with Sierra, just sit there, talk to her, and keep her company. But I had to let it go for now. I had to understand where she was coming from. I had to be patient. "Tomorrow then."

Anna and I met Ron and a few other volunteers at the shelter the next day. It was a beautiful morning and if I ended up inside for the next few hours, I didn't care. In fact, I was going to try and stay most of the day. I knew Ron had to be at rehearsal at one, so Maureen could use the extra help anyway. Besides, that way I could spend some quality time with Sierra without Ron watching my every move. The only clincher was my mom wanted me to help out with her open house from one to four in the afternoon. I would just have to be a little late. I knew once I told her about Sierra, she would understand.

Both my parents were huge animal lovers. They actually rescued a lab-hound mix right before they got married. My dad said the three of them went everywhere together. Even on their honeymoon. I've seen all the pictures, and in every one, Abby had top billing. My mom even got her approved as a therapy dog with a vest that said, "Pet me. I'm friendly." So whenever my parents traveled on the airplane, Abby could sit with them up in the bulkhead and not down in the cargo hold, where God knows how loud, or cold, or hot it got. My mom said she would never make that mistake again.

One Christmas, before Abby's official rank as "Therapy Dog," my parents had to fly down south to spend time with my dad's folks. The airline assured my mom the baggage area was temperature controlled and completely safe for family pets. "Never again," my mom repeated. When they arrived in New Orleans and saw Abby's kennel come out of baggage claim, she knew something was wrong right away. She was lying down and coughing up phlegm. My dad said the kennel was ice-cold. They immediately took her to the local vet where she was diagnosed with kennel cough and pneumonia. After four weeks of antibiotics, absolutely no exercise, and the loss of fifteen pounds, Abby recovered. My mom on the other hand was about to sue. Instead, she got a note from a friend's psychiatrist, whom she met with for thirty minutes. It stated that due to separation anxiety, (my mother's, not Abby's) it would be harmful to my mom's health and state of mind should she be prevented from traveling by air with her dog at her feet.

In all the photos, it looks as if Abby is grinning, with her big tongue hanging out, knowing full well she was one lucky dog. With my mother's arm wrapped around her large furry body, and my father's arm wrapped around my mom, love connected the three of them.

When Abby was diagnosed with lymphoma at the age of nine, my parents decided to do everything they could not to prolong her life for their sake, but to keep her as comfortable as they could for as long as they could. It was Thanksgiving morning when Abby couldn't walk over to her bowl for breakfast. My mother hand fed her. "She ate," she told me. "She even wagged her tail with each morsel of food I picked out of the bowl, but I knew. I knew our time together was coming to a close. I woke up your dad and we took her an hour away to the best vet possible."

"But why?" I asked. "I mean, isn't putting a dog to sleep pretty much the same in every vet's office?"

"I don't know, Case. And I didn't want to find out. I knew our vet, the one Abby had been seeing for the treatments, knew how much we loved her. I also knew the doctor would administer anesthesia first and then the poison that would put our girl to sleep forever. Without anesthesia, an animal could suffer before the heart completely stops. Even though it is quick, I wanted to be certain that our sweet girl would be pain free as she crossed over."

After Abby died, my mom got pregnant with Patty. I asked her why they never got another dog. She told me they wanted to devote their free time, what little they had, to fostering dogs from high-kill shelters, and finding homes for them. But my dad said, saying goodbye to Abby, and watching your mom kiss her snout while the injection was given, was worse than taking a beating. They just didn't want to go through that again. He had never seen my mom so beaten down. When Abby's heart stopped, he thought for sure my mom's would as well.

My dad told me that mom and Abby had been best friends and went everywhere together. My dad too, but he worked pretty long hours and didn't have the luxury of taking Abby on the long hikes in the hills that my mom did at the time. I knew she would really take to Sierra and understand why I wanted to help change her life.

The first hour at the shelter was spent cleaning the cages, feeding the dogs and cats, and making sure all the animals had fresh water. I asked Ron how Sierra had been getting exercise. He said she hadn't. As far as cleaning her cage, it was just a matter of him going in there while she crouched in the corner. "So, you're going inside," I said. "How come I can't?"

"Because, I'm bigger than you."

I wanted to say *not by much*, but I didn't think that would go over too well. Ron was an interesting guy. He had more of an artist's body– slim but strong. I had seen him haul bags of food as if they were filled with feathers and not fifty pounds of grain. He just kept going without breaking a sweat. Either he really loved what he did, or he had a cape hidden somewhere. Maybe it was both.

"Besides, it isn't so much going inside. It's what I'm afraid you'll do once you get in there."

Ron was right. Unless she was snarling and showing her teeth, it would have been hard to keep my distance. Hopefully, I wouldn't have to worry about that for long.

Anna and I were outside in the yard, watching a group of dogs running around, chasing after each other and jumping in the baby pool that Ron had picked up at the local Walmart. Anna had a grin as wide as the one she wore when we were bellowing out *"Grease is the Word"* before the 'Saturday sabotage' took full effect.

"Thanks, Casey."

I knew what she meant. Watching these dogs run around without risk of being hurt or facing hunger was a happy feeling. What was even better, you could almost sense how grateful they were. As if they knew those bad days were over and this was their celebration.

"Almost as good as being up on stage, isn't it?" I said.

"Better," Anna replied.

"Yeah, look at them." Two of the dogs came prancing up to us, playing tug of war by holding opposite ends of a thick rope in their mouths. One end had a rubber tennis ball, the other a big tied knot. "Our standing ovation."

Ron walked into the yard. "So what are you guys up to?"

"Well, one thing we're not up to is going to rehearsal," Anna said.

"I know. That completely blows," Ron said.

"It's okay. This makes up for it," Anna said, as we watched the dogs running around after each other, chasing their tails, rolling on their backs in the grass, flying in and out of the pool and shaking water off their coats.

"I thought Anna and I would hang with Sierra for a bit." I knew this would ring Ron's mental alarm, so I grabbed the rope with the attached tennis ball, swung it high in the air and tried to distract him with the beautiful dog show.

"Okay, just go slow, Casey."

"I know, I will." I said, without looking his way.

"All right, I'll come back at five to give the dogs dinner. It's a nice day. You can leave them outside till then. Just make sure they have plenty of water. If you're around when I get back, I could use some help, if not, I'll see you whenever you're here next."

"Oh, I'll be around," I said.

Ron laughed. "At this rate, your hours will be finished by next week."

"Then you can hire me."

"I hope I can," he said, while sprinting off to the parking lot.

"What did he mean by 'go slow?'" Anna asked.

"He just worries that I don't think things through sometimes."

"Funny, where would he get that idea?"

I wanted to give Anna a few hours to get used to the shelter before taking her to see Sierra. It was pretty sad to have a beautiful dog in such a state. With everything Anna had been through, I didn't want to push her. I walked toward the pool and dumped out the muddy water, put the hose inside, and turned on the nozzle.

"So when can I meet Sierra?" Anna asked.

"Now, if you like. But just know that things are going to get better for her."

"Casey, I'm not as soft as I look."

"Good, cause I'm not as tough as I look," I said.

We headed back inside and passed by Maureen. She was brushing Tango, who looked as if she was getting a massage, stretched on her back with pleasure.

"Going to introduce Anna to Sierra, if that's all right?"

"Oh, sure. She'll warm up eventually. She's just being cautious. It's hard to know exactly what she's been through. But dogs let things go a lot more quickly than us stubborn humans. You'll see."

Anna and I passed by empty kennels since most of the dogs were outside. And then, there she was, in the last one drinking from her bowl. Once she spotted us, she leapt off to the far side and started shivering with fear.

"Oh, no," Anna said, as she crouched down to Sierra's level. "It's okay, girl." We just looked on, feeling completely useless, while trying to coax her with soothing words that had no meaning for her. "She needs a good cry and someone to talk to."

That gave me an idea. "You're right. She needs a buddy. I know what I'm going to do."

"Something, please," she said.

"I'm going to bring Shiloh in from the yard and see how she reacts."

"Can you do that?"

"Yeah. There's an exit right on the side here that goes directly outside. I'll bring him in that way."

"No, I mean, don't you think the staff would have already tried an interaction with another dog if it was safe?"

"What staff? It's basically Maureen, Maureen's daughter Peggy, whom I haven't met yet, Ron, a Vet Tech who comes once a week, and a few volunteers. I mean, what can it hurt?"

"You could lose your job."

"This isn't a job. It's technically one level shy of a prison sentence."

"Some prison sentence. You look pretty happy to me."

"I'll be even happier once she is," I said, while pointing to Sierra. She was curled up in the corner of her kennel with her nose facing away from us. "I can't take this. We're only stressing her out more. Let's go get Shiloh."

We walked into the yard, and many of the dogs were lying down in the grass, bathing in the sunlight. All of them ran up to greet us. One tan-colored hound dog, with his tongue and tail flapping from side to side, did a circle around my legs, then jumped up on my knees as I squatted down to scratch behind his ears. Shiloh was a lover.

We gave out turkey jerky to the other dogs, then I led Shiloh around to the rear entrance on a leash. I walked him over to Sierra's kennel. She was still in the far corner, but as soon as she saw Shiloh, she sat up and stared, checking him out without giving us the snake eye. Shiloh jumped up on the kennel with his tail wagging and then dropped down on the ground trying to sniff under the opening. Then magic happened. With head down, Sierra cautiously made her way over to his side. I let go of his leash and Anna and I took a few steps back. The howling was music. Shiloh and Sierra were licking each other through the openings in the wire. I looked at Anna, who was open-mouthed and shaking her head with happy disbelief.

"Do they know each other?" she asked.

"They do now."

Sierra got on her back and started kicking her legs in the air, with one paw on the cage, where Shiloh had mushed his head.

"Okay, now what?" Anna asked.

"When Ron returns later, I'll tell him what happened. Hopefully we can bring Sierra out in the yard with the others." I looked at my watch. It was close to 2:30. I was really late to help my mom and I totally forgot to call. "I have to go. You want to meet back here later on?"

"I can't. My mom and I are having a girl's night out with two of her other friends from the hospital. Besides, I think that Ron wouldn't mind hanging with you by himself."

"Please, I'm just glad that Shiloh and Sierra hit it off."

Shiloh was lying down right outside Sierra's kennel with his nose up against hers. "Nothing like a good friend to help you forget the bad," Anna said with a nudge to my shoulder.

"Okay, so I'll talk to you later. Thanks for the help."

"Right back at ya," Anna said.

Anna walked out the front entrance, leaving me holding Shiloh's leash. How I was going to find the heart to break up these two, even temporarily, was not going to be easy. I was so tempted to let Sierra out in the yard, but I just didn't know how she would behave with the others. Patience, Casey, patience. I brought lover-boy back outside, grabbed my backpack from the closet, and took a look at my phone. No messages from my mom, which was odd.

I jumped on my bike and headed up Pinehill Drive, then over three more blocks to Bayberry Circle. This was the high-dollar neighborhood of Riverton, and was actually where the Bradboy and Sinister Cindy lived. The homes were mostly old Tudor style, three-story estates with at least an acre of property serving as land moats surrounding the homes. This new listing was a real score for my mom, and when I rode through the gate up the very long driveway, I was surprised to see so many cars. I knew open houses brought in a few people, but not this kind of crowd.

Uh, oh. Then I remembered. I was probably so busy mulling over my lost role, and summer, that I didn't get the importance of this one particular open house. This wasn't just your regular mid-income event. This was a catered affair that brought in some potential buyers, and buyers' agents, who had money to burn. The lump in my throat grew even larger when I saw the van that read 'River Market Gourmet.' My mom was probably so busy fielding questions, handing out listing information, giving tours of the house with all of its amenities, and playing hostess, that she didn't have time to text to find out where I was.

I walked in and immediately felt all eyes on my shorts and T-shirt that had smudges of slobber, food and dirt. I wasn't quite sure how I smelled, but I'm pretty certain it wasn't sweet. My mom came out of the kitchen holding a tray of food. She walked over to me and said, "Go home, wash up, change, then have your dad drive you back here ASAP."

I did an about-face and retreated out the door. I jumped on my bike and raced down the steep driveway. The wind had picked up, so I needed to get some good speed before heading against it up the next hill. I took the sharp turn by the gate a little too fast. That's when I almost smacked into a woman who was parked around the corner. She was fixing herself in the side window of her Mercedes sedan and had to veer out of my way, losing the scarf she was wrapping around her neck. I grabbed it with one hand before the wind took it too far, then circled around. I rode by and passed it back to her. "Here go. Sorry about that." I pretended not to notice the purplish rash she had been trying to cover up with the scarf.

When I walked in the door, my mom must have called my dad, because he was waiting in the hallway. "Sorry," I said, as I ran up the stairs two steps at a time.

"Ten minutes, Case. In the car in ten minutes," he said.

"I can just ride back."

"No. We need to bring over more ice and glasses." Stuff my mom would not have run out of if I had been there to help her.

I ran into the bathroom and threw cold water on my face, ran a brush through my hair. *Ouch*, that is until it got caught on a large stubborn knot underneath my right ear. I tugged and tugged until a wad of it came out into the bristles. My hair was showing some streaks of auburn because of the sun and I decided to wear it loose for once and not restrained by a rubber band tucked under my baseball cap. I threw on a sundress and sandals, and borrowed my mom's pinkish lip-gloss. I ran downstairs to the kitchen and started to help my dad wrap up glasses in a box. He looked at me and paused mid-motion.

"You okay?" I asked.

"Wow, honey, when your mom sees you dressed like that, you'll definitely make up for being so late. What's the occasion?"

"Dad, you should have seen all the imported cars lined up in the runway outside that huge home."

"That is quite a house. Well, she deserves it. She's worked her tail off."

"I know, and I want to help her more. I have just been really busy at the shelter. Maybe I can get a job there after I've served my time."

"Our little jailbird."

"I'm serious. I think I'm pretty good at relating to these dogs."

"Remember the time when we were in the woods behind our house and you found those two baby squirrels that must have fallen from the nest? Their eyes were still closed and you nursed them back to health with an eyedropper and some formula we picked up from the vet. I thought for sure I'd have to fight you to set them free. But you smiled through your tears when they chased each other up a tree in our yard."

"There's this dog at the shelter named Sierra. I know you and Mom would fall in love with her."

"Your mom is even more crazy about dogs than I am. But right now, I think she has her hands full. Besides, even though it's been a long time, I don't know if she wants to go through that again. She was pretty beaten up after we lost …" Dad looked at the clock. "Oh, hey, we have to fly. Just grab that bag of ice. I've got the glasses."

When we arrived at the open house, the driveway was even more crowded then before. We parked in the front, by the porte-cochere, and brought our supplies through the garage and into the kitchen. My mother was speaking to the same woman I almost took out as I was testing my Tour de France skills. This time her scarf was elegantly hiding the mystery marks around her neck. She was there with another middle-aged couple.

"Oh, there they are," my mom said, as she waved Dad and me over. "Guys, I want you to meet Alice Bender and her clients, the Albertsons."

No, there was no way that this stylish, poised lady was related to the same Cindy Bender. No way. Then again, maybe that wasn't a rash, and those bruises came from somewhere, or someone. *Okay, calm down, brain.* My dad walked over and shook all three hands, and gave my mom a kiss on the cheek.

"Nice to meet you," I said, while keeping myself busy by setting up more glasses and cleaning up the table.

"Please, Alice, show your clients around the garden in the back. I'll be giving the tour shortly," my mom said, then walked over to me. "Wow, you're finally wearing that dress we bought you three years ago. You look like an angel. That hair of yours, you should wear it down more often."

"An angel? Right."

"To me, you are."

"Well, if that's Cindy Bender's mom, I can tell you right now, I'm no angel as far as she's concerned."

"That is, and you are."

"Why are you so calm? I've killed a potential sale."

I could tell my mom was preoccupied with how busy it was getting and needed to work the room to do her meet and greet. For the first time ever, I even detected a little stress-breath on her. She was really hyped up, talking quickly, but softly, which wasn't easy for her to do. "Alice Bender got into the real estate business about nine months ago, after she and her husband separated. She also has an only child, a daughter a year older than you: and yes, her name is Cindy." I must have been catching flies, because my mother added, "Close your mouth, she has no idea about you and the cobra."

"Cobra? Jesus, Mom. Who do you think I am? I didn't want to kill her."

My mom waved to another couple and their agent who just walked in. "Honey, I've gotta run. Can you bring out more strawberries and brie? Where's your father?" We both turned around and saw he was still out in the garden, talking with Mrs. Bender and the Albertsons.

"Oh, God, Mom what if Dad says something about me pulling that prank. That would be really embarrassing right now."

"Honey, Alice Bender, unless she has a really good poker face, has no knowledge of what happened that evening. I don't think her daughter ever said a word. In fact, I don't think she knows what kind of reputation her daughter has about being a bully. She thinks she's an angel." Mom grinned while squeezing my nose.

"Ow. Then you two are the lobotomized Stepford moms of Riverton. But what if dad says something?"

"I don't think that's information your father wishes to voluntarily share, no offense."

"None taken. Okay, go do your thing." She headed into the crowd of guests. "Oh, Mom?"

She turned back around quickly. "Honey, I have to go."

"Mom," I said, while blowing my breath into my cupped hands. "You need some gum, no offense."

She covered her mouth and her eyes got really big. "Get me some," she whispered.

I also wanted to tell her what I saw around Mrs. Bender's neck, but she got called over by a tall dark-haired man in a double-breasted Armani suit. He air-kissed my mom and led her up the stairs with two other men wearing designer flip flops, linen shorts and polo T-shirts. I turned to see my dad making his way back into the house with Mrs. Bender. I did a quick turnaround and made myself busy in the kitchen for the next two hours.

After everyone left, I emerged with dishpan hands and a full stomach. My father was disassembling the large serving table, and my mother was at the front door saying goodbye to a Fredrik look-alike from *Bravo's Million Dollar Listing.*

After another air kiss, she closed the front door with a hand swipe across her brow, grabbed the bottle of wine off a table, and poured two glasses. She handed one to my dad and clinked his with a toast. "I have not one, but two, offers. Let the bidding wars begin."

"Congratulations. That not only calls for a toast, but dinner out. How about we pick Patty up from work and grab some of Monte's great fish and chips down at the harbor?"

I held my stomach. "You guys go. I overdid the cleanup in more ways than one."

"Too much brie, I bet. And that was the triple cream kind," my mom said.

"You're not helping."

"Oh, sorry, sweetie. Go home and put a hot pack on your stomach. We won't be late." She gave me a kiss and big hug. "Thanks for all your hard work, and the gum."

"Sorry I was late, but Mom, I want to tell you about this dog. You have to meet Sierra."

"Your dad already mentioned it. Honey, if I walk into that shelter, I'm walking out with a dog, and I definitely can't handle that right now."

"I can take care of her. I'm doing it now."

"And who's going to take care of her when you go off to school?"

"That's over two years from now, and who even knows if I'm going to college."

The pin dropping on the floor was heard around the neighborhood. "Just kidding. I'm going to school." Mom's expression relaxed and I gave her a playful bump. "Come on. Just meet her."

"We'll see. But right now, I'm starving, so let me call the owners with the good news and get out of here."

I decided to walk home to give my stomach a breather. I was going to tell my parents about Alice Bender, but I wanted to talk to my older sister first. Patty often had a tendency to have a mental marathon when it came to her personal life, but for the past two summers she had been interning at the Riverton Times and was great at taking a pretty impartial view of even the most obvious stories. For all I knew the marks could have been a rash, but I didn't feel comfortable ignoring it. Still, I wanted to slow down and not jump to conclusions this time. The last thing I wanted to do was spread dark rumors, even about Cindy. But I knew my curiosity would get the better of me and I would google 'parental abuse AND teen' when I walked in the door.

I was lying on my bed reading *Bruiser* by Neil Shusterman, about a sixteen-year-old loner who emotionally absorbs all the pain and anger of those he loves. The compelling twist was that it physically manifests itself in the form of welts and bruises on his body. The whole subject started me thinking, when my sister walked in.

"How was dinner?" I asked.

"Great. You feeling better?"

"I'll live."

"Good, 'cause we brought you some leftovers."

"Ew. Not that good."

"Hah, I've been there. At least you're in the comfort of your own room. It's the worst when you're out with someone."

"No, I can't imagine that would be a good date night."

Patty took a look at my book. "Oh, that's a good read. I love his stuff."

"I like it. It's pretty disturbing though. You think it can happen?"

Patty sat down on the bed. "You mean the injuries? Yeah, I think it can in theory, or maybe not even in theory. I think people can make themselves physically sick by taking on too much and holding pain inside. Whether or not the bruises actually show up on the body, I don't know. In many ways, what's the difference?"

"Do you know anything about Cindy Bender and her family?" I asked.

"Only what you told me about her being a total jerk to your friend. I was already in college when she was a freshman. I know a little bit about her parents though. Why?"

"I met her mom today, Alice Bender. She seems really nice. Nothing like Cindy."

"Maybe a little too nice."

"What do you mean?" Then, after some obvious reluctance, Patty spilled the beans.

"Alice Bender was married to Dr. Alan Bender. Last summer his name came up when I was writing the police blotter at the paper."

"Police blotter? What's that?"

"It's basically an update on all of the arrests or charges the police have made in the last week. Most of the arrests have to do with DWIs or teenage vandalism. I remember the police went to the Benders' to investigate some domestic abuse calls. It was strange to me, because in a town like Riverton, you wouldn't think that would happen at all, let alone as many times as it did from the same household. What was also surprising was that the charges were made against the husband, who happened to be a respected doctor. After the third incident, Mrs. Bender finally issued a restraining order."

"Yeah, well, maybe good ole doc isn't honoring it."

"That doesn't surprise me, but why do you say that?"

"I saw her earlier this afternoon. She was trying to wrap a scarf around her neck when she had to jump out of my way. It was pretty windy and it flew out of her hand. She had these marks on her neck that looked like bruises, but I could be wrong. I just caught a quick glance."

"You sure?"

"It was pretty obvious. Like I said, it could have been a rash."

"Maybe, but with their history, it's unlikely. One of the articles I worked on last summer was about a law that had just been passed. Domestic violence had been treated too generally, as if it was all just a slap in the face. Not that a slap should be taken lightly, but there can be different degrees of severity. So it was decided that something as serious as choking should be considered second-degree strangulation, with a sentence of up to two years in prison."

"How much time would they serve before...?"

"It depends. In some cases, it was considered a misdemeanor, with as little as no time, or a few months. In the Benders' case, it never even got that far. When the police came to the house for the third time, Mrs. Bender was coughing up a storm and could barely speak. That's usually a sure sign there was severe trauma to the throat. But the bruises don't show up right away, and she denied strangulation. Whatever he did, it obviously got her to finally file a restraining order and separate from the guy. She probably didn't want to put him away for two years, just wanted to keep him away from her."

"I guess, but choking someone, that's really serious. You could kill a person."

"That's precisely why they changed the punishment to fit the crime. But if what you saw were bruises, she has to say that he really tried to strangle her. She has to press honest charges this time."

"That's what I don't get. She seems like a strong, smart person, who wouldn't let anybody do that to her and then get away with it."

"Remember, she did file a restraining order. And after this, I'm sure she'll file for divorce."

"I just can't understand why she never told the police what he really did. Maybe she is too nice."

"I shouldn't have said that. He's the father of her daughter. It can't be easy. If she presses charges this time, he would most likely go away for several years."

"But if he tried to kill her. I don't know. It's just too weird. Maybe we're missing something. Maybe she's not being truthful about it because it isn't him. Maybe she's covering for someone else."

"For whom?"

"For Cindy," I said. My sister gave me that look of hers that allowed me the time to rethink what I just said. "It's possible, Patty. You know she's a bully. And, I looked it up online. There were a lot of search results having to do with teens inflicting physical abuse on their parents. It's called "silent abuse" because parents don't want to rat out their kids."

"You actually think Dr. and Mrs. Bender would go through the charade of a separation and a restraining order as a cover up?" Patty asked.

"Yes, for a daughter who has a problem. I think a parent would take the fall."

"I highly doubt that, Casey. That's one heck of an accusation and I wouldn't make it lightly. I think you need to step back and let Mrs. Bender take care of this one. She's an adult and has plenty of money. She could hire a good lawyer if she wanted. Unfortunately, there are many women who don't have that. Hard to believe, but she's one of the lucky ones."

"That is kind of hard to believe."

"What I mean is that I've reported on cases on the outskirts of my college town where the women don't have any resources like Mrs. Bender. Those women are stuck due to economics. Alice can get out if she wants."

"You think it's that easy? What if it's her daughter who's doing it? How do you put a restraining order on your own child?"

"That gets a little more complicated," my sister said.

"Yeah, well, leave it to Cindy to complicate things."

"Turn your imagination down, little sister, and try and dream like you don't have to save the world tonight. I have an early morning interview, so see you tomorrow. If I get off early, maybe you can introduce me to Sierra. If you're there, that is."

"Oh, I'll be there."

"I figured that. I'm proud of you for taking this and turning it around for yourself."

"Hopefully, I can help turn it around for the dogs. Hey, maybe you can do a story on the shelter, talk about what the animals have been through."

"That's a good idea. I'll run it by the editor. Goodnight, Case."

"Night."

I turned off my light and rolled over on my stomach. It was beginning to soften and now felt like I had wet cement in there and not a hard brick. I just can't eat like I used to.

The next morning, I was helping my mom at her office. She had just landed another listing and wanted me to head over and take some pictures so we could load them up on the web.

"It's a short sale," she said as I was heading out the door. "Just take a few good photos that show the home in a good light. The owners won't be there, so go inside with the key in the lock box. Here's the combo."

My mom handed me a slip of paper. "What's a short sale?" I asked.

"It's when the owner sells their property for less than what is owed to the bank. The bank then forgives the rest of the loan."

"Why would a bank do that?"

"It's usually because they think they might lose less money on the house."

"Yeah, I didn't think it was because they were being kind and considerate."

"Well, honey, it is a business. But I know what you're saying. Many people were lied to about the mortgages they were sold."

"We learned a little bit about that at school."

"We're coming out of this financial meltdown, but for some it's still a nightmare." The phone started ringing. "Okay, ride safely and see you back here for lunch."

I headed out the door and jumped on my bike. Other than lifting bags of dog food, and a few dogs, I hadn't had much time to work out these days, so I wanted to pump my legs as hard as possible while I rode. I started thinking about what my mom said. I didn't quite understand why the crash happened. I did know a lot of people lost their homes and jobs. Through all the complicated muck, it was simply unfair, and yes, ironic that even though taxpayers had helped out big banks, banks were now unwilling to return the favor.

I made my way down the side street to a neighborhood quite different from the other day. Homes were much smaller, yet the lawns were still impeccable. There was definitely pride of ownership here. I saw the modest ranch at the end of a cul-de-sac and rode into the driveway. I walked up to the front door and knocked, just in case there was someone inside. No answer. I retrieved the key and opened up the front door. Wow, it was nice: small, open and elegant. The light through the rear bay window shined on the oak floors. The mantle on the small stone fireplace had many tastefully framed black and white photos of an attractive man and woman at their wedding, big smiles beaming. I took out my camera and had turned to take a picture of the green lawn through the back window when a woman's face appeared in the frame. I almost dropped the camera.

"You're Karen's daughter," she said calmly.

"Yes, I'm Casey, agent assistant and office photographer. I'm sorry. My mom told me to use the key in the lock box and let myself in. No one answered when I knocked."

The woman was around my mom's age. She wasn't wearing any makeup, which probably would have helped cover the large shadows beneath her eyes. Still, she was naturally quite pretty. She wore blue jeans and a silk shirt, with large turquoise earrings that you could just make out through long chestnut hair with streaks of gray. Definitely the one in the photographs from several years ago.

"No problem. I just came here from the bank. I left your mom a message. There won't be a short sale."

*Hmm? Okay.* Because I knew there was more to the story behind that remark, I decided to wait through the uncomfortable silence for an opening. When none came, I blinked first. "That's good, right?"

"Good for the bank. They think the market is coming back, so they'll foreclose on the property and sell it for more than we can get now. They win. We lose. Same old story. They're too big to fail, we're too small to win."

Just then, my phone started ringing. "Excuse me." I saw it was my mom and answered.

"Hi, honey," she said. I could tell she was rushing, and driving, at the same time. It seemed as if she had been trying to make up for all the business she lost a few years ago and was now running on pure adrenaline and anxiety. "I'm sorry. I probably shouldn't have let you go over there by yourself in the first place. I guess I've been overwhelmed lately. I wasn't thinking clearly. Are you okay? Is Mrs. Callahan home?"

"Yes," I said. "I'm coming back now."

"Okay, let her know I'll call her later on this afternoon."

I was trying to sound professional. "Very good. I'll do that. 'Bye." I hung up and turned to Mrs. Callahan, who was now in the kitchen, pouring a glass of something. I couldn't blame her for needing a drink. A foreclosure sounded pretty ominous. I remember the fights my parents had over possibly losing our home and having to move in with my grandmother down south. It was obviously time for me to go, even though this woman seemed pretty cool and calm over the whole thing. "Okay, well, my mom said she would call you later. I have to get back now, so good luck with everything."

"It's pretty hot out there. Want a glass of iced tea before you leave? It's really good. I put fresh mint in from the garden and local honey from our neighbor up the street. They harvest their own from the beehives in the yard."

Not that I should care whether this woman got a bit buzzed in the afternoon, but I was relieved she wasn't starting her cocktail six hours early. "Sure, thanks, Mrs. Callahan."

"Just call me Susan."

I never called anyone my mother's age by the first name, but what the heck. "Oh, okay, thanks, Susan." She handed me a glass, and she was right. I was pretty thirsty and this stuff was awesome. "Wow," I said. "This is amazing."

"It really is. And if you have allergies, the local honey really boosts your immunity."

"I don't, but good to know, I guess."

"That's good. My husband suffers from really bad ones. Sinus mostly. But, we couldn't care less about that now."

I wasn't quite sure what she meant by that so I kept my mouth shut.

"Have you been working with your mom long?" she asked.

"No. This is the first summer. She got her real estate license a few years ago, right before the market went into a tailspin. Now that it's picked up, she needs the help."

"My husband and I bought this home right before the crash. Saved up for years. It was our first home. Then he got cancer, lost his job, medical bills started piling up, and we just had more going out then coming in."

The words coming out of Susan's mouth didn't match her mood. It all sounded pretty dismal, but she seemed rather matter of fact and accepting of it all. I wasn't quite sure how to respond, except to say the obvious. "I'm sorry." I really hoped the guy hadn't died and didn't want to ask.

"Oh, it's okay. He's doing great now. There were a few tough surgeries and some rough recoveries, but the doctors say he is pretty much out of the woods. He's working again. Loves his job. Losing this house doesn't concern us."

"It's a nice house," I said.

"We'll find another one when it's time. I'm just happy I still have Cal. That's my husband."

"Yeah, I saw him in the photos. He's handsome."

"He still is. Especially now that he put some weight back on, after all those rough chemo treatments. He couldn't keep anything down. But that's all over." She noticed my glass was empty. "Want more tea?"

"Oh no. That was delicious, but I should get back before my mom starts to worry. So, are you going to move out of the area?"

"Just down to the city. We scored a great one bedroom in Morningside Heights. Cal is a teacher in the Bronx. I'm the school librarian there. He's just filling in for someone who's on maternity leave, but the kids love him, so I think it'll all work out. What am I saying? It already has."

"What do you mean?"

"He's healthy. That's all I need."

These weren't empty words. This woman was losing a home that she had put her spirit into, but she knew it was all just stuff. She had her man and that's all she cared about. It looked as if she was tired of worrying about all the silly things that didn't matter. Her face was worn out, but she was calm and beautiful.

"I should take off. Thanks for the tea." I got up to leave.

"You're welcome. I would say I'd see you again, but I think that's unlikely."

"Hey, you never know. I do like the city." I opened the front door and jumped on my bike.

"Us too. Be well, Casey."

"'Bye, Susan. I'd say 'good luck,' but I think you already have that."

"Yes, I do. Lots of it."

I made my way back to my mom's office and was in a pretty good mood myself until I heard the yelling from outside. I walked in and caught my dad and mom in the middle of pretty loud fight.

"I made a mistake, John, all right? Haven't you made a few yourself?"

"Not when it comes to our daughter's safety."

"What's this about?" I asked. "I'm safe. At least I think I am."

"Casey, you are never, ever to go to a vacant house by yourself again. Never. Do you hear me?" my dad said.

"It's kind of hard not to hear you, Dad. I think the entire complex hears you right now."

"Don't be fresh."

"Well, don't be so loud."

"Okay, John. It's over now. She's fine."

"Maybe you need to pull back a bit, Karen. Slow down," my dad said.

"Slow down? Are you serious? We're just now beginning to get out of debt and, need I remind you, that if you hadn't left your secure job to go out on your own, maybe I wouldn't have to work so hard and have stress cloud my judgment."

"You know perfectly well that wasn't my fault. I didn't cause the market to tank."

"Oh, my God. Only other people are ever at fault. You're never guilty of anything." My mother's face was crimson and I was sure the cops were going to arrive any minute. If they did, I hoped to God it wasn't the same officer who brought me down to the station. Some family we were. "No one put a gun to your head to leave the agency, John. That was your decision and no one else's."

"You know why I left. I couldn't stay there with that CEO who was born with a mutant gene of toxic narcissism."

"Sounds contagious," I said, trying to melt the ice that had formed in the room.

"It's why I left," my dad said.

"No, you couldn't stay there," my mom said. "I get it. I supported you in that. But you're not supporting me now."

"Not supporting you? I praise you and what you've done. I just think you've gotten a little self-involved with your work and sometimes don't think of how it affects others."

Uh, oh. My mom looked as if she was going to blow. The veins in her neck started to swell as her eyes locked in on my father. I thought they might glow, like Storm in X-Men, with bolts of lightning striking out. "Get out of my office before, I swear to God, I scream so loud the walls come down."

I knew my mom was tired and stressed, but I had never seen her like this before. I flew out of the room, jumped on my bike and headed for the shelter, fast becoming a refuge for me as well as the animals. I didn't feel the heat as I was pumping up and down the hills. I was soaked with sweat when I rode into the parking lot. I walked right past Ron and the dogs in the back yard, grabbed the hose and doused myself with the cool water.

"You look as if you just completed a triathlon."

I took a drink of water. "I'm going to get a towel. I'll be right back." As I walked back inside, I tried to calm my breathing down. My cell phone was ringing. It was my mom. I didn't pick up. I grabbed a towel from the back, dried myself off and read her text.

> I'm sorry you saw that. I'm sorry I lost my temper. What I do, I do for the family. I hope you see that.

I put the phone down and grabbed a dry T-shirt from storage, then went back outside to tell Ron about Shiloh and Sierra. When I arrived in the yard, he was standing there holding Shiloh by a leash.

"Going somewhere?" I said.

"We are, the three of us. Back inside to get Sierra."

"You know what happened?"

"I do."

"How?"

"Maureen."

"Maureen? She didn't see us."

"Maureen sees everything. Actually, she was surprised she and her daughter hadn't thought about it before. Then again, they've been pretty busy trying to save the entire shelter. Thanks for taking a chance."

"I thought you'd be angry at me."

"You promised you wouldn't go inside her kennel. You didn't. You brought another dog to her, outside her kennel. And it worked."

"I just hope it helps her feel safe with humans too."

"Let's give it a try. I'm going to bring the two lovebirds to the larger yard in front. Have her let out some steam. She's been cooped up for too long now. Then, we can introduce her to a few others, one by one."

We walked back inside and brought Shiloh right up to Sierra's kennel. Their noses met through the wire and their tails started wagging furiously. As soon as we opened the door, Sierra bolted to the back corner, leaving Shiloh pawing the wire.

Ron released Shiloh's leash and he flew toward the back where she was crouched down. They started rolling around and jumping up and down, while singing their happy, high-pitched whines.

"I'm going to open up the side door to the front yard. When I say so, just call Shiloh while running outside. Hopefully, he'll chase after you and Sierra will follow him out to the yard."

"You got it," I said.

Ron jogged out through the aisle, and then I heard him call, "Okay, Casey."

I opened up the kennel door and began to run back out. "Come on, Shiloh. Come on, boy." I kept running and made it to where Ron was standing by the gate to the yard. We didn't hear anything at first, then we heard the scraping of nails on the tile and Shiloh flew past us and into the outside yard. He turned back around as if he was looking for his companion. When she didn't come, he flew back inside. Then we heard it. Loud running and barks of delight as the two of them rounded the corner of the building, Sierra playfully biting Shiloh's fluffy tale.

They looked like gazelles prancing around the perimeter. Sierra was completely unfazed by Ron and me standing there. He threw a ball high in the air and Shiloh chased after it. Sierra didn't really know what to do, so she just kept close to Shiloh, that is, until he came back to Ron and dropped the ball at his feet, so he could toss it again. She just retreated to the center of the yard and kept her distance.

"Why don't I get the other dogs as a distraction. She obviously doesn't have a problem with them, it's just us humans," I said.

"Well, she doesn't have a problem with old lover boy here, so why don't you bring in one of the males, maybe Diesel. I doubt there will be a problem with him. Even, if there is, it'll be really quick to break up a fight with just the two of them by using the hose."

Ron let Diesel into the yard. He was a beautiful black Rottweiler with white around his muzzle and a laid back soul. He trotted right up to Sierra and Shiloh with a goofy grin on his face. When Ron threw the ball, Shiloh took off with a much slower Diesel running behind. Sierra just watched, then chased off after them, not to retrieve the ball, but just to join the party. We brought in a few other males to keep her as top female of the pack and prevent any jealousy issues. One of them was an adorable Benji look-alike, who kept chasing after her tail.

Sierra was getting all the attention and having the time of her life. Still, whenever I walked up close to pick up the ball, she ran away. After about forty minutes of the dogs flying around the yard, they were pooped, and lay down under the tree. I made my way over to Shiloh and started rubbing his belly. I put the leash around his collar and started leading him around. Sierra just watched me walk away with her pal.

Then, with her head down, she began to follow about ten feet behind us. The others stayed put and just rested with their big tongues hanging out. I continued on while Sierra followed, with Shiloh constantly turning around to make sure she was still with us.

At the far side of the fence up a small incline he sat down and I joined him. Sierra stopped as well and just stared at us, still keeping her distance. We were there for almost an hour. Then Shiloh lay down and put his head on my lap. I started scratching behind his ears, and stroking his head. He continued to focus on Sierra, who was now lying down as well.

"Come on, Sierra. Here, girl." Shiloh's ear perked up on this command and, as if he was urging her on, he started to bark. Sierra slowly started making her way over. She got close enough so she could lie next to him. She was about two feet away from me and I could just lean far enough over Shiloh and softly touch her fur. She didn't move. I inched myself closer, so I could stroke her head, and then lightly scratch behind her ears. She bent her head back and rolled on her side, so I could get even closer. It was as if she hadn't felt a warm human touch ever, and she softly exhaled with comfort and peace. I sat with both dogs next to me until the sky began to light up with warm reds over the river. I looked up and saw Ron walking over with an even warmer smile.

He was careful to give us a wide berth as he walked around and sat down next to me on the other side. "What next?" I asked.

Ron handed me a collar. "Why don't you see if you can take your hand around her head and replace it with this."

As I rubbed Sierra's head with my right hand, I held the collar in my left and slowly placed it around her neck. She looked up at me. "Good girl," I said.

Ron gave me the end of her leash and he took Shiloh's. "We should head back. You walked quite a bit."

"I know, but she followed."

"She needed the exercise. She should sleep well tonight."

"She's not the only one."

Ron gave me a hand up and the four of us headed back to close up the shelter for the night. Sierra stayed close to Shiloh, and as long as we kept walking, she didn't pull away. Ron, Shiloh and I brought Sierra back to her kennel. I really wanted to bring her home. Actually, I wanted to bring both her and Shiloh home, but Ron told me that a family was going to come by tomorrow who had an interest in adopting him. I was thrilled, but not happy for Sierra. I brought her some food and fresh water and sat down in the far corner of her kennel while waiting for Ron.

She was still wary of me, but as long as I didn't make any sudden movements, she would eventually warm up to my reaching over and petting her head. She loved to be scratched behind the ears and would slowly submit to leaning over on her side to be closer to me.

Ron showed up. "Well, don't you two look comfortable. You're pooped, huh, Sierra? Good girl." And then it happened. Maybe it was Ron's voice, meant to offer comfort and peace, as well as the head massage I was giving her, but her big, bushy tail tapped her pillow twice.

"Did you see that?" I asked.

I looked up at Ron and he was beaming. "That a girl, Sierra." I wanted to give her a kiss on her snout, but that would be pushing it. "Pleasant dreams, sweet girl." I slowly crawled over to the door. "See you tomorrow." And then her tail did another thump on the pillow as her eyes closed. Hopefully, her dreams of chasing rabbits had begun, and her nightmares ended.

Ron put my bike in the back of his pickup and drove me home. We parked on the driveway and listened to the crickets begin their chorus. A warm breeze blew through the car windows and I was self-conscious of the fact that I had been running around with dogs all day and hadn't even showered. Ron was pretty grubby as well, but, as usual, guys always get away with what girls can't.

"See you tomorrow?" he asked.

"Absolutely. I have to help my mom in the afternoon, but I'm going to ask her about adopting Sierra."

"Really? I thought your parents would give you a definite 'no' on that one."

"Maybe, I don't know. I have to try. They seem to think *they*'ll be left with taking care of her when I go off to school."

"Well, they're right about that. She can't be more than three years old. But you could always foster her. Give it a try and see what happens. Your folks will probably fall in love with her and not want to give her up."

"Yeah, but there's no way I could give her up if they eventually say no."

"You really think that's going to happen? Besides, if you tell them it's only a foster, without a commitment, maybe they'll say 'yes' initially, and then won't be able to say 'no' later."

"I'll give it a shot. Thanks."

"It's nothing. It's just an idea."

"No, I meant for helping me salvage my summer."

"I don't think I had anything to do with that."

"If you hadn't introduced me to Sierra, this would not be one of my banner summers."

Ron looked outside the car window, as if he was taking a moment before speaking again. "Quite frankly, Casey, If I hadn't met you, this wouldn't have been mine either."

I was taken completely off guard and had one of my rare moments of not knowing what to say. I felt my face grow warm when Ron turned back around to look at me with a serious, but kind, expression. He put his hand on my cheek, and started to lean over to me, when I heard our front screen door open up.

"Casey, you want to invite your friend in for dinner?" I looked through the windshield at my dad, standing right outside on the front porch. An apron was tied around his waist, and since he had shorts on that you couldn't see, (at least I hope he had shorts on) it looked as if he was wearing a skirt. Two large oven mittens were on his hands. With one, he held the screen door open. With the other, he was holding a large spatula the size of a badminton racket. What a vision.

I was surprised Ron didn't jump, or pull his hand away from my face, when we heard my father's voice. He was so cool and calm about it. Almost as if that's what we were meant to be doing right then and there, like there was nothing wrong with it. Not that there was. I mean, I was sixteen, he was eighteen, and this is how things were supposed to progress, right?

"Meet my dad. The cute guy in the cuter skirt."

Ron smiled and got out of the car. The two of us walked up the driveway. Ron put out his hand and shook my father's. "Hi, Mr. Riley, I'm Ron."

"Nice to meet you, Ron. Care to join us for some barbecued chicken and the works?"

"My dad is quite the cook."

"I'm sure, and it smells pretty awesome from out here, but I'm expected at the theater in half an hour."

"Oh, that's right. I completely forgot about the play."

"Forgot about the play?" my father said. "I didn't think I'd ever hear you say that."

"Believe me, neither did I."

"Well, listen. It was nice meeting you. I've gotta fly, but thanks for dinner."

"Another time." My father went back inside and I turned to Ron.

"Okay. So, I'll see you in the morning then?"

"You'll see me in the morning." Ron made that grin again, which I both loved and hated at the same time, then got in his truck to drive away.

I walked inside. My father was in the kitchen slicing up mushrooms. "Where's Mom and Patty?" I asked.

"They went to the movies. Should be home in a bit. You didn't respond to your mom's text. You okay?"

"I think the more appropriate question is, 'are you and Mom okay?'"

"Your mom and I will always be okay, sweetheart."

"She was pretty angry. I can't say I blame her, Dad."

"Nope, I can't say I blame her either. I didn't mean it the way it sounded. I think your mom knows that."

"I don't think Mom is selfish."

"I don't think so either. She's concerned."

"Concerned about what?"

"Well, honey, we owe a lot on this house. Patty has another year at school and you're going off to college in a few. Your mother has this fear that she'll end up like her parents, with little to live on in her old age. Your mom is one of the most beautiful people I know and would give her right arm to protect her kids, but right now, she's so stressed out about our finances that sometimes she can't think straight. She certainly doesn't sleep at night."

"I didn't know it was that bad."

"It isn't that bad, sweetie, but your mom thinks it is. She's running herself ragged so we can get this house paid off faster, and give you girls as much as we can."

"I don't need anything. Well, actually that's not entirely true."

"Well, what your mom needs right now is to relax a bit more."

"And I know just the thing to help get her there."

"You do, huh?" We heard the car pull into the driveway. "Well, I'm hoping this meal and her favorite bottle of vino will help. Can you grab it out of the fridge, honey, and bring the corkscrew?"

I walked into the kitchen while my mom and sister were heading inside from the garage. "Hi, how was the movie?"

My mom was shaking her head in that way she always does when she is without words. "I loved it. The book was better, but wow, Viola Davis was incredible."

"Isn't the book always better than the movie?" I asked.

"Not necessarily," my sister said. "I actually liked the movies *Fellowship of the Ring* and *The Two Towers* better than the book."

"That's because you like Viggo Mortensen and hate fantasy fiction," I replied.

"Well, I like having a fantasy about him," my sister said.

My father walked in and gave my mom a hug. "I know who I like to fantasize about."

"Gross," I said. "That could mess a kid up."

"Too bad," my father said, and gave my mom a warm kiss on the cheek. He then pulled the wine out of the fridge and grabbed two glasses.

"Oh, my favorite. I hope you didn't pay too much for that?"

"I don't remember." And with that, my father took my mom's hand and headed out to the porch to see the amazing sunset. My sister turned to go upstairs.

"Patty, you coming out? I need your support on something."

"What's that?" she asked.

"Just something to help mom chillax a bit more."

She knew full well what I wanted to do. "Why don't you just bring Sierra home. I'm sure once Mom meets her, she'll melt."

"I don't know if Sierra's quite ready for that yet, but she will be soon."

"Well, I suggest waiting until she's ready. Then just lay it on Mom without asking. She's wound a bit too tightly right now to say yes to anything."

"I thought we could foster Sierra for a bit. So Mom doesn't feel the pressure of committing."

"I think that's a great idea, but again, I would wait until Sierra is ready. Okay?"

"Okay."

"I'll be down in a bit. I just have to finish this article by tomorrow morning."

"What's it about?"

"Keeping the Riverton Retreat open."

"The one for battered women and their families."

"That's the one."

"Like Alice Bender?"

"Like Alice Bender. And you helped me come up with the idea. It actually does involve her, but in a good way."

"Casey, can you bring the corkscrew?" my dad called out.

"Coming."

"You'll read about it in the paper if I get it finished in time."

Patty headed upstairs, and I went outside with corkscrew in hand. I knew my sister still struggled with finding a way to make a difference, but she was doing it. She did have a mission and I was really proud of her. Now, if I could only make sense of mine.

By the end of July, I had completed my one hundred and fifty hours of community service. It really didn't matter. I was planning on staying to help out anyway. The shelter was getting over crowded. Times were still tough for many people. Pets weren't cheap and often they were the first to go in a pinch. We were seeing a lot of owner surrenders and abandoned dogs. The good news was the town had reached an agreement with a local philanthropist to privatize the shelter. Ron said she was an heiress to some international food chain and was a huge animal lover. "You actually know her mother," he said.

"Her mother? How do I know her mother?"

"Because her mother is Maureen Kelley," Ron said.

"Maureen is an heiress to a multi-million-dollar company?" I couldn't believe it. Maureen was one of the most natural, unpretentious earth mothers I had ever met—moving heavy bags of food, using a pooper-scooper, and mopping up animal pee without a whimper.

"It's actually her late ex-husband's company, so I don't know if she's technically the heiress, but her daughter Peggy is."

Peggy Kelley was all about equipping the shelter with a full time, top-notch trainer to rehabilitate dogs with behavioral issues, as well as reaching out to the community to promote responsible adoption. She also wanted to hire more full, and part-time, staff. I was hoping to be on that list so I could spend more time there, and less time at my mom's office. My dad was right. What I'd thought was going to be a summer of enslavement turned out to be more freedom for Sierra and me.

Now, whenever I approached her cage, she jumped up and ran over to the door, wagging her big bushy tail in anticipation of our walk through the meadow. Shiloh was happy in his new home and, fortunately for Sierra, the young couple who adopted him brought him over on the weekends so they could have a play date. But, as we watched him get in their SUV and drive off, with his nose and mouth slobbering up the back window, I knew the time was coming when I would have to bring Sierra home as well. I wasn't worried about anyone adopting her out from under me. She was still really skittish around strangers and not many people wanted to deal with that, especially when it came in the form of a massive canine like Sierra. But it was becoming more and more difficult to latch the door on her kennel at night. I knew what she was thinking as she stared at me through the wire, with a tilt of her head and those amazing crystal eyes: *What are you doing? This place isn't bad, but isn't your bed big enough for the two of us? I mean, come on already.*

I had to time Sierra's release just right, when my mom would be the most receptive. Lately, I wasn't sure when that would be. The real estate business was struggling to pick up. With that came a lot of competition. Recently, I walked into the office when Mom was red-faced, yelling into the phone.

Some broker had lowered his commission and stolen a big client from her after she had wined and dined them, as well as spent countless hours coming up with a successful marketing plan for the property.

So, I just didn't want to guilt her into a corner when I brought Sierra home. She had a big heart when it came to dogs, but these days, she also had a short fuse. Can't say I blamed her.

Short fuses seemed to be a thing of the times. Many people were so freaked out about money and they took it out on the ones closest to them. At least that's the reason why my sister was writing a series of articles about the need for more funding for the family refuge downtown. It had opened last year and was already at a hundred percent capacity. Patty wrote that all families fight, but it can get worse when people are underwater financially. It reminded me of a remark that John, the vet tech, said to me one afternoon when I first started working. He had lost his job and health insurance at a big veterinary practice about eighteen months ago and still hadn't found steady work. I was complaining of the dog poop in the yard and how it just kept piling up. "It's hard to keep on top of it," I told him.

He laughed. "Well, at least you can get rid of poop by just tossing it in the garbage. But man, when you have debt, the interest alone just keeps adding higher and higher to the pile till you can't see around it." I hoped that John would get hired full time. He needed that, and the animals certainly needed him.

I read Patty's first article: *When Hard Times Hit, the Hitting Gets Harder.* It was really good, and profiled these women who, without the shelter, had no place to go, except to stay with their abusers. Unfortunately, the shelter was also facing hard times and the economic recovery wasn't fast enough for those needing to recover. But, as I soon learned, though money might help, it didn't always ensure safety.

When I came back from my walk with Sierra. I strolled into the lobby and saw two women standing with their dog. They were talking to Maureen. I knew who they were.

Cindy Bender held the leash of a beagle-boxer mix, curiously sniffing the cage that housed our guinea pig, Elmo. With his positive attitude, Elmo was our shelter mascot. He was munching on a carrot and not the least concerned about the dog's white and black snout exhaling a sauna into his home. Standing next to Cindy was her mom, Alice. There was a side of me that wanted to grow up, say hello, and walk right by them through the door into the kennels. It was easier to be a coward. I retreated and was about to go through the back entrance. That is, until I heard part of the conversation.

"I'm so sorry, but we're overcrowded as it is. Unless it's an emergency, we just can't fit 'owner surrenders' anymore," Maureen said.

"Define emergency?" Cindy asked, with her winning 'tude.

This could be interesting. I took a deep breath and, with Sierra as my support, walked up to the desk. "Hi, Mrs. Bender."

"Oh, hi, Casey. Beautiful dog you have there. Do you work here?"

I wasn't about to explain the backstory of why I was here. If Cindy knew, and happened to tell her mom, so be it. I had served my time and was moving on. "I'm one of the volunteers."

"Casey is a huge asset," Maureen said. "As soon as the new management organizes the staffing, she'll be a paid employee."

"Here's hoping, Maureen."

"Oh, I think it's pretty much a done deal. We just have to finalize with the town what their share of the bargain will be. They own this building and I think they are going to let us stay here rent free, which is a huge help."

I was trying to avoid looking up at Cindy, so I focused my attention on her dog. "Who's this?" I asked.

"Roscoe," said Cindy.

"Oh, hey, Roscoe." Sierra was already on her back, pawing up at him and making him feel right at home. Dogs did have a way of melting a thick slab of ice. "Is he yours?"

"He was. We're trying to find a new home for him," Alice Bender said.

"A safe home," Cindy added.

There was an epic behind that remark. I exchanged a look with Maureen. "I was just explaining how we can't accept owner surrenders at this present time," she said.

"Which is why I asked, 'define emergency,'" Cindy repeated in her typical smartass way.

"Be polite," her mother said.

*'Be polite?' How about just be normal.*

"No, it's okay. I understand the frustration." Maureen turned to Cindy. "In some cases people have had to give up their animals due to economic hardship, like losing their home. They are known as 'foreclosure pets.'"

Maureen was quite the cool cat. With the Gucci bag that Alice Bender was holding, and the newest iPhone 4 Cindy was fixated on, she knew that was most likely not the reason. Cindy just needed a little perspective thrown her way, or so we thought.

"It's rather complicated, and personal," Alice Bender said.

"Of course," Maureen said. "And we don't need to know the details. So if it's an emergency, then by all—"

"Here we go again," Cindy said, after exhaling a burst of air. God, I hated it when people huffed like that.

This was getting really uncomfortable. Fortunately, Roscoe and Sierra were now jumping over and around each other, as if they didn't have a care in the world. Cindy and I were trying to give them as much freedom as possible without letting go of the leashes. Sierra was so much bigger, but was instinctively playing lightly with her much smaller friend, hopping over him and tenderly nipping at his neck. They were pretty adorable with one another and it was hard to keep a straight face in light of the weirdness of this visit. The reading on the Geiger counter was falling.

"What's your dog's name?" Cindy asked.

"This is Sierra. I'm hoping she'll be mine soon."

"I love her eyes."

"Amazing, huh? Funny, it looks as if they've known each other forever. Where'd you pick him up?"

"My mom found him on the side of the road a few months ago. My dad's allergic."

I'd say. Seeing the colorful *choker* he'd recently given his wife made me realize that allergic reactions came in all shapes and sizes.

Then I had an idea. "Maureen, I'll be right back. I'm going to take Sierra and Roscoe into the back room so they can let off some steam together?"

"Good idea," Maureen said, with her cute thumbs up move.

I walked Cindy back to the large playroom. It was just an open area with an empty floor except for a few beds and toys. "You can unleash him and they can just run around." Cindy sat down in the corner and took out her phone while I filled up a bowl with water. "I'll be right back," I said. She didn't even look up.

Maureen was sitting behind her desk, alone. "Where's Mrs. Bender?" I asked.

"Using the bathroom. That is one upset woman. Do you know what's going on with that family?"

"Not really," I lied. "I was thinking. At least for tonight, or until the dust clears, why don't we put Roscoe and Sierra in the same kennel? They get along with each other really well, and he's pretty small."

"Yes. We can totally fit in another bed and that will give us, and them, time to figure it all out."

Just then, Alice Bender came out of the bathroom. It looked as if she had thrown water on her face. Her makeup was pretty much washed away. I could also tell she had applied fresh lipstick.

"Alice, we have a temporary solution that might help," Maureen said.

"Really?" Mrs. Bender said, while looking at me with some relief.

"I'm going to tell Cindy," I said as I walked back.

I was about to enter the room when, through the window of the door, I saw that Cindy had lost interest in her phone. She was hugging Roscoe, and planting her face in his. Sierra was lying down next to them.

Knocking was silly, so I just walked in. When Cindy looked up, it was pretty clear she had been sobbing her eyes out. I pretended not to notice, though I'm sure she wanted me to. It was probably easier for her to explain her situation physically than with words. What better way to get sympathy? Man, I had gotten pretty cynical.

Feeling like an idiot, I clapped my hands like a cheerleader. "So, considering how well these two behave with one another, we thought we'd let them have a sleepover for the next few nights." No response. "That'll give us time to work it all out." Cindy continued to embrace Roscoe tightly, while Sierra was trying to nudge her nose in on some of the cuddling. "Sound good?"

"Whatever," Cindy said through a stuffed up nose and a coat of Roscoe's fur.

"Well, I'll just meet you guys up at the front desk whenever you're ready. Take your time. Come on, Sierra, here girl." Sierra jumped up and headed toward me.

"You're lucky, you know," Cindy said.

I heard her, but wasn't quite sure how to respond. "Sorry?"

"You heard me."

"You're right. Not about the lucky part. Well, perhaps about that, but I did hear you. I just didn't know what you meant. We're all pretty lucky, I guess."

"Says who?"

"Well, there are people who have it a lot worse. People who can't pay their bills and are losing their homes. And animals are feeling it too."

"They aren't the only ones feeling it."

"Well, no, in fact, my sister just wrote an article...." I stopped myself, realizing the subject might hit a little too close to home, literally.

Cindy looked up with a red, blotchy face and swollen eyes. "You know what they say about money."

"They say a lot of things about money."

"It doesn't buy happiness."

About ten minutes later, Cindy brought Roscoe out to the lobby. I told her to come back tomorrow if she wanted to see them playing in the yard. She said she was busy, so I just let it go. Maureen told Mrs. Bender that she would let her know what the new private administration would decide. What I didn't tell Maureen was that I had already decided.

When I walked in the door around 4:00, I heard a drilling sound coming from the kitchen. At first I thought my father was just finishing up some Saturday chores, and then I walked in and saw our new addition.

"Dad, is that what I'm hoping it is?"

"Is it large enough? I got the biggest doggie door in the store."

"How'd you know?" I asked, knowing that Patty had probably said something to pave the way.

"Your sister told me."

"I'm glad, but I don't know if this is the best way to go about it. Mom might not be too happy about what you did to her kitchen door."

"It's just a smaller door on a larger one. Besides, your mom couldn't care less. All she cares about is the dog getting out and having a good quality of life without her having to do it all, especially now that she's working seven days a week. Come on, let's go back and get Sierra."

What timing. I was so happy, but at the same time feeling a large pit taking up space in my stomach. I didn't want to separate Sierra from Roscoe so soon. When I left them in their kennel, they were sharing her big bed, and he was using her stomach as a pillow. I almost saw one corner of Cindy's mouth moving up in a slight smile.

"You see, Dad…"

"Aren't you happy, honey? I thought you'd be thrilled."

"I am, totally. It's just, well, Sierra's in love."

W e walked into the shelter right when Ron got back from rehearsal, busy closing up with two other volunteers.

"You just can't get enough of this place, can you?" he said, showing off that crooked grin of his.

"Neither can you. Dad, Ron basically runs the place."

"Not for long. It looks as if I'll be second in command until I start college in four weeks." Ron shook my father's hand. "Hi, Mr. Riley, nice to see you again."

"I guess that means the staffing is moving along?" I asked.

"Yeah, it is, which is really good news. I'm pretty certain they'll be able to hire you and Anna as part-time kennel assistants. Peggy Kelley is actually here now with one of the full time animal trainers she just hired. The dude has a degree in animal psychology and worked with Cesar Millan out near Los Angeles."

"Who's Cesar Millan?" my dad asked.

"The 'Dog Whisperer', Dad," I replied.

"Oh, right, the show you and your mom love to watch."

"Peggy has taken over temporarily as shelter supervisor until they hire someone," Ron said. "Then she'll be busy doing what she does best, keeping the money coming in and the dogs moving out to good homes. She's also hiring John full time, as well as getting a retired vet to come in two days a week, pro-bono."

I was so happy for John. It was so obvious he loved what he did. "That's great news. He's the best."

"What about recovering the animals running around loose?" my dad asked.

"Well, that'll continue to be managed by the town's department of Animal Control," Ron said. "It's a safety issue. I've met the head of the department, Dave Sanders. He's not a bad guy. It's just, he's been operating for the last two years with little to work with. Now that the town will be spending hardly any money on caring for the animals, they'll have more to pay staff, and correctly run a department that can safely get lost or abandoned pets off the streets…"

"…and into our hands," continued a woman who had come into the lobby from the kennel area. Peggy Kelley looked to be in her early fifties, with short blonde hair. She could have been Martha Stewart's twin, wearing a blue chambray work shirt with an expensive leather belt synched around her middle, high brown leather boots and form fitting jeans. She had Tango on a leash, and a young man was following her with one of the other dogs who had recently been surrendered to us. I had seen him in the back kennel and was, quite frankly, scared to get close. Samson was a very large male pit bull with a terrible scar on the right side of his face where his ear had been bitten off. The sister of a guy who used the poor animal as a "bait dog" in an illegal dogfighting gambling ring had brought him in. The police had since closed it down and many of the dogs had been adopted. Some of them, like Samson, were still too dangerous to release into a family home and needed to be rehabilitated.

"Oh, hi, Miss Kelley. This is Casey Riley and her dad," Ron said.

My dad shook her hand. "John Riley. Nice to meet you, Miss Kelley. Looks like you've made some great changes around here." Tango was already pushing his head into my hands so that I could give him an ear scratch. The trainer commanded Samson to sit down and wait a few feet behind us.

"Please, call me Peggy, and yes, we are off to a good start. Thanks to Ron and my mom, as well as all the volunteers like your daughter. We still have a lot of work to do, but they have all kept this facility operating quite well under the circumstances."

"Samson is looking good." I meant it. When I first saw him, he would not stop snarling or jumping up on his cage whenever anyone walked by, man or beast. But now he was sitting there, albeit a few feet away, calmly and patiently.

"He's doing much better," said the young guy holding the leash, gently petting Samson on his very large head. He leaned over and shook my hand. "Jorge Ramirez, nice to meet you. I've heard you're to be thanked for doing such a great job with Sierra. Looks like you might have a future as a dog therapist."

I continued to pet Tango. "Well, I don't know about that, but I sure like doing it. In fact, that's why we're here. We came to bring Sierra home with us for good."

"She's all yours. And if you want a job working here after school, you'd be training with the best," said Peggy. "Would you like that?"

"That would be awesome. Did Maureen fill you in on Sierra's roommate?"

"She did. So, do you happen to know what's up with Cindy and her mom?" she asked me.

"We don't, Peggy," my dad said. "But we'd like to help out if we can and keep Roscoe with us until you find a home for him."

"Sure, like a foster. We can do that."

"Cool. I figured it would work," I said.

"So your mom said yes?" Ron asked.

"We haven't asked her yet."

"But how can she not?" my dad said.

"**M**om, we can do this."

When we heard my mom's car pull up, my dad and I had left Roscoe and Sierra playing in the back yard. We walked into the kitchen, where she was pulling a bottle of white wine out of the fridge. She looked beat. "No, Casey, you can't, and therefore, *we* can't."

I was hoping that once she saw Roscoe and Sierra running free outside, it would be canine therapy. It didn't even get that far.

Her eyes were bloodshot and had huge dark moons beneath her lids. For the past several months she'd been juggling several high-dollar listings. One had sold well below the list price, which she had tried to explain to the sellers was way too high in the first place. Buyers were still wary about sinking their life savings into a shaky housing market. Even those sellers hoping to just break even had unrealistic prices in their heads. My mother was one of the few honest brokers out there, trying to tell homeowners what they could expect from a potential sale. Many didn't want to hear the facts because it meant less money in their pockets, or in worst cases, more money owed to the banks. So they went to the brokers who gave them pie-in-the-sky figures. Initially my mom understood. Some owed more on their homes than they were worth and were praying to cut painful losses. Their fears of financial loss made many tough to deal with. Tempers and anxiety were flying high. My mother's cell phone would go off late in the evening and she would listen to nasty tirades from her clients, as well as from her competition.

After five months of advertising one particular home, tirelessly hosting many of its open houses, and showing it to an endless supply of potential buyers, the seller cancelled the listing contract with her and went with another broker who charged less in commission and promised he could get more for their house. She lost time, money and much sleep. The home was still on the market, and now listed at less than what a potential buyer had offered months ago. That buyer happened to be a client of my mom's, and had the seller accepted, she would have raked in the listing agent's commission as well as the buyer's commission. "It would have paid for Patty's last year of college," I overheard her tell my dad last week. I listened for the all too familiar sound of ice cubes and gin rattling around in a shaker, which came every evening now around 7:30. The seller accused her of double-dipping and not representing his needs ethically. Or, as my mother put it to my father between sips of a double martini, she was not meeting her "fiduciary responsibilities." He'd threatened to bring her up on charges in front of the real estate board if she didn't release him from his listing contract with her. It was a tough business made tougher by people's situations. She was putting way too much pressure on herself just to make money. There had to be another way. Seeing her in the kitchen now made me realize she just wasn't cut out for this cutthroat environment.

"Babe," my dad said. "Why don't you put on your jeans, pour yourself that glass of wine, and come outside and sit with us while we watch the dogs run around."

"Oh, so they're here already?" Our nervous silence was her answer. She didn't even bother to look out the window. "Thanks, you two. Thanks for consulting with me first. No pressure now." She turned to my father and I held my breath. "You know, the other night, you said I was drinking too much. So which is it, John? Or do you just want me to drink when it serves your purpose?"

"Mom, come on, relax, Dad just wants you to enjoy life a little more."

"That costs money, honey," my mother said rather sarcastically, "and right now we don't have enough to even pay for Patty's last year. So your idea of not wanting to go to college, Casey, is a welcome one. You don't have to go."

"Karen! Cut it!" my dad said.

"Let me ask you both something. Why am I considered the bad guy here? Because I'm the only one to shed light on the truth? And you two, who live in a dream world of rescuing dogs and 'enjoying life,' are rather selfish." How rescuing dogs became a selfish act was an astounding notion to me. My mouth must have been wide open again. "Close your mouth, Casey. And yes, selfish, because I know the reality."

"I know the reality too, Karen."

"No, John, you don't. You think you do. I was home more, and saw more, when Abby got cancer. I don't blame you for that. You were working fourteen-hour days and couldn't be around her as much as I was. But right now we're both working all the time, and it still isn't enough. How can we give a life to a dog when we don't have a life ourselves? Dogs are expensive when they get sick. And, unless they're suffering, you shouldn't just do what's convenient, or jump to putting them

121

down, like many people do. Those people who want the selfish gratification of seeing that adorable muzzle lying next to them while they read a book, or sleep with them at night, are unwilling to go the distance when that drool turns bloody, or they mess all over the house because they have bladder cancer. Dogs are part of the family and keeping them healthy costs money, and that, sorry to be the bearer of bad news … No, correction, facts, the bearer of facts. We don't have any to spare right now!"

I looked at my father and he had tears in his eyes. It was the first time I had ever seen him cry. My mother was ranting, but what she said made sense in a sad, angry sort of way. She sat down on the kitchen chair and finally saw the doggie door. I thought she would hit the friggin' ceiling. Then I heard the beginnings of a chuckle. She started laughing, then really laughing. She was laughing so hard, and loudly, I thought she would fall off the chair. My father was crying, my mother was laughing, Roscoe and Sierra started howling loudly outside, and I was going to be one messed up adult.

My mother stood up and walked out the kitchen door. She sat down on the steps off the deck. Roscoe ran up and into her lap, dropping the large stick right before he took out one of her plants lining the stairs. Sierra took advantage of Roscoe's distraction, picked it up and took off with it. "You dropped the stick, buddy, get the stick, where's the stick?" my mother said, while she rubbed Roscoe behind the ears and scratched his neck. He started making that deep hound-dog bark. Sierra was keeping her distance from my mom, but prancing around proudly, waving the stick in her mouth like a baton twirler in a parade, taunting Roscoe to come chase her.

My dad and I walked outside. I went into the yard and called Sierra. She ran over and gave me the stick. I tossed it high in the air for the two dogs to race after it. I turned around and my dad was sitting next to my mom with his arm around her.

"Your dad tells me it's only temporary. Roscoe that is, not Sierra. Sierra you're planning on keeping."

"Only if it's okay, Mom. I don't want to stress you out anymore. I get it."

"That's not the dogs' fault. Just because we allowed ourselves to be screwed, doesn't mean we should screw these dogs. They had nothing to do with any of this cash-strapped crap. So, it's not okay."

"Wait, what's not okay?" I asked. My mother had lost me once again.

"It's not okay that we just keep Sierra. Having two dogs is easier. They keep each other company. I'll feel better knowing they are together and not lonely when we're gone for twelve hours a day." My mouth must have been wide open. "Honey, you're catching flies again, close your mouth."

My dad gave my mom a big smooch on the cheek and I fell down on the grass with Roscoe and Sierra slobbering over me as well.

Anna came over for dinner that night. It was amazing outside, dry with a warm breeze. All of us were hanging out on the back deck, watching Sierra jump after fireflies. Roscoe sat on the ground, staring at her with his head cocked, waiting for her to lose interest so they could chase each other around the yard, or from the looks of him, fall asleep together. I hadn't figured out how both of them were going to fit on my bed, but that was a happy concern.

"It's pretty amazing how well they get along. As if they've known each other longer than a few hours," Anna said.

"Who knows?" Patty said. "Maybe they lived next door to each other at one point."

"I doubt it. Sierra was chained up most of her short life," I said.

"Maybe he visited her when he ran away, or was let go," Anna said.

"Maybe. But they'll both have a good life now. I just feel bad for Cindy and her mom."

"Did I hear you correctly?" Anna said.

"Yeah, you did. You should have seen how upset Cindy was, saying goodbye to Roscoe."

"Then why did they give him up?" Anna asked.

"I have an idea. It looks as if Dr. Bender was fired from his medical group last week," Patty replied.

"How do you know that?" my mother asked.

"You know I did those articles on the Riverton Family Retreat. One of the big donors happens to be Alice Bender. I've interviewed her a few times and gotten to know her pretty well. She's one of the reasons why the facility has been able to stay open."

"What does that have to do with Dr. Bender and Roscoe?" I asked.

"Remember when I was writing the police blotter last summer and there had been several 911 calls from that house?
"

"Yeah, Mrs. Bender finally got a restraining order on him, but from what I saw, he wasn't sticking to it," I said.

"You were right, Casey. Money might make a bad situation easier, but it doesn't make it easy. The guy has a really bad drinking problem, but had gone to AA and apparently had it under control, so Alice Bender took him back."

"That must have been right before I saw her outside Mom's open house. Bad move, Alice."

"Casey, honey, as your sister said, it isn't easy. Marriage is complicated," my mother said.

"Mom, from what I saw, that isn't complicated. That's pretty cut and dry."

"What do you mean?" my mom asked.

"We're pretty certain that Dr. Bender put his very strong hands around his wife's throat," Patty said.

"Oh my God," my dad said. "You mean he tried to kill her?"

"It doesn't matter if he just intended to scare the hell out of her. The fact is, he did, and it wasn't the first time," Patty said.

"She never should have let him come back in the first place. What was she thinking?" I asked.

"Well, there's obviously more to this story, and I think for us to try and assess what really happened when we weren't there is a little judgmental," my mom said.

"Mom, I saw what he did and it wasn't pretty."

"But from her perspective," Anna said, "what if it looked as if he solved his problems and stopped drinking? Alcoholism is a sickness, right? If you love that person, you may want to give them more than one chance and try to help them. My dad was sick for a while. My mom made his last few months with us so much better. She was always there for him."

"Not if they're trying to kill you. Your dad wasn't beating your mom," I said.

"No, he wasn't. It was hard though. Really, really hard on her."

"Anna, I don't think there's any similarity there," I said.

"The fact remains," Patty, said, "she did take him back, and the bottle didn't stay closed for long. His partners were concerned about malpractice, or worse. With what you saw, Casey, I don't know why she didn't have him arrested this last time. But she was the one who spilled the beans by calling the hospital last week when her husband was on his way to surgery. He wasn't drunk yet. But he was really hung over and sick as a dog. Present company excepted, of course."

"So where does Roscoe fit in with all of this?" my mom asked.

"Well, there was another 911 call to the station a few days ago. This time Alice wasn't the one calling. It was Cindy," my sister said.

I wasn't too happy with myself right now for thinking Cindy could possibly be behind her mom's chokehold.

"According to the police report, the 911 tape revealed Cindy's voice crying out for help, saying her father threatened to kill her mom's dog," Patty said.

"What a guy," my father said sarcastically. "Pillar of the community."

"Well, that's what's so strange," Patty said. "He always had been until he started drinking a few years ago. Alice told me that the pressure to make the medical group more profitable, with longer hours, less time for patients, greater number of mistakes, and higher malpractice costs, was just too much for him. What started out as a drink or two to chill out when he got home became three or four, and not just after he left for the day."

"Maybe that's why she got her real estate license. To support the family," I said.

"No, she always wanted to work, but never needed to financially. You know, her dad owns that organic food company out in Ohio. The woman is loaded. But she started showing homes before her husband had his breakdown. Said she loved it, and it was obvious from how well she did, and her reputation," my sister said.

"Her clients love her. She really goes out of her way to help, and not just on the million-dollar listings," my mom said.

"After she started doing well, and he was sliding, Dr. Bender got really jealous. She could handle the pressure, but he couldn't."

My mom picked up the bottle of wine to pour herself another glass. "Well, she's a lovely woman. But there really is no 'pressure' when you don't need to work in the first place." She saw me staring and put the bottle back down on the table without a refill.

"He accused her of showing him up. The 911 call came last Wednesday evening after Alice phoned the hospital 'ratting him out,' as he put it," Patty said.

"The next morning is when they came to the shelter with Roscoe. She and her mom looked pretty beaten up. Not literally, but well, you know what I mean. The two of them couldn't stop crying. Now I know why," I said.

"I don't know about all of you, but I feel pretty weird talking about them like this," my mom said. "This is way too private."

"Well, honey, if we're going to adopt Roscoe, we should know the backstory. We're not judging or criticizing them," my dad said.

"No, but I did," I said.

"I think you can cut yourself some slack on that one," said Anna.

"So what's the deal, Patty? Where is good ole doc now?" I asked.

"No one knows," Patty said. "After Cindy made that call to the police, he took off and hasn't been seen in a week. Alice had the restraining order reinstated and is now filing for divorce," Patty said.

My mom took a big sip of wine. "That's creepy."

I nodded. "Well, hopefully he's gone for good."

"Unfortunately, that's not usually how these situations turn out. He'll be back in some form or another," Patty said.

My mom got up and put her empty glass in the sink. "Or, maybe he's getting clean and sober."

"Either way, if he does return, Roscoe won't be getting in his way, will ya, boy?" I looked over at the two dogs. They were pooped and lying in the grass next to each other with fireflies sparkling around them.

"Roscoe won't. But what about Mrs. Bender?" Anna asked.

*And Cindy?* I thought.

I t was pouring. The streets going to the shelter had streams on both sides. My mom drove me over for my first morning as a paid employee. She was happy to release me from my real estate office duties, which made me feel super guilty.

"Mom, you need me. I can totally help out for a few more weeks until school starts."

"No, Casey. You're doing what you love to do and making money while doing it. What more can I ask of my daughter? I'm so proud of you. It's not fair that I stick you with helping me do something I'm not even thrilled about doing myself."

"Then why do it, Mom?"

"Sweetheart, I felt the same thing about working at the advertising agency where your father and I first met. I was good at it, but I hated it. My happiest days were being with our dog, Abby, and then Patty and you. But I have to make a living. I can't throw it all on your dad. That's not fair, and I'm afraid these times don't allow many people that luxury anymore."

Just then I saw Peggy Kelley's Range Rover splash through the puddles and park next to us in front of the shelter. She got out of her car and waved at me, then sprinted inside the building without an umbrella.

"Is that the new owner?" my mom asked.

"Yeah, that's Peggy Kelley. She doesn't want to be thought of as the owner. More like the sponsor. She's cool. You'd like her."

"It's not easy what she's doing. But if she knows the right people, she can keep animals safe and warm for a long time. You just have to get out there and do a lot of promoting and awareness. Something you would be really good at," my mom said.

"Actually, that's something you would be great at."

"Well, it's what I did at the ad agency. I just wasn't overly turned on by what I was selling."

The idea hit me so hard that my eyes felt like they were popping out of my head. "Oh my God, Mom!"

"What, what is it, honey?"

"That's it. That's what you could do. Peggy Kelley is looking for a shelter supervisor. She's only doing it now until they find someone permanent. She wants to free herself up so she can reach out to the community, raise money and wine and dine deep-pocket donors."

"Honey, I don't know anything about managing a shelter."

"Yes, you do. You love animals. You're smart. You know how to encourage responsible ownership. You know how to advertise and get these animals adopted into loving homes. It's perfect."

"I'm certain Peggy Kelley has a lot of candidates with far more experience than me."

"I don't think it's about that, Mom. It's not about experience for her. It's about passion and love, and you've got that. Just come inside. Just meet her."

"I won't do that, but I will call her about it, okay?"

"You will?"

"I will."

"When?" I asked.

"Oh, Casey, later this afternoon, but don't get your hopes up."

"Me? Never."

The rain had stopped and the sun was beginning to break through the clouds. Jorge came out into the wet yard with Samson and Tango.

"What beautiful dogs," my mom said. "Pit bulls get such a bum rap."

"I know. I was one who thought that way. It's unfair. It's not the dogs' fault. It's what people do to them."

"Damn shame. Who is that young man?"

"That's Jorge. He's one of the trainers Peggy Kelley hired. The bigger one, that's Samson, he's been known to be pretty aggressive— not with people, with other dogs. He seems to get along well with Tango there, so it's a start."

"Well, when you've been trained to fight for your life, all your life, it's hard to know who means you no harm."

"You want to meet him?" I asked her.

"I'd love to, sweetie, but I don't think it's a good idea to interrupt. Besides, you should get going."

"I'm way early." I got out of the car and waved to Jorge.

"*Buenos Dias, Senorita* Casey. *Como estas?*"

"*Estoy bien*. How's Samson doing?"

"So much better. He just needs to shake off those demons a little more. He'll get there."

"Guess we all will eventually, right, Jorge?"

"You're way too smart for a young girl, you know that?"

My mom got out of the car. "Couldn't agree more, Jorge."

"Jorge, this is my mom."

"Hi, Mrs. Riley, nice to meet you."

"Please, call me Karen. That is a beautiful tan boy you've got there. Kind of like Daddy."

"You know Daddy?"

"Not personally, but I watch the show pretty religiously. I hear he has cancer."

"Yeah, Cesar is very upset about this."

"I understand. These dogs get into your soul. When they leave us, it rips you up inside."

I noticed Samson's short tail started to wag once my mom started talking. I think Jorge noticed this.

"*Si*. Why don't you come over and say hi?" Jorge said.

"Come on, Mom. Just for a minute. "

"It looks pretty muddy out there, sweetie, and I have a meeting with a buyer in an hour."

"So, go home and change your shoes."

"I have a feeling I know where this is headed."

"Then why fight it?" I asked, realizing I was beginning to sound like my mom.

"Sure, why not."

My mom and I walked through the fence into the yard. She walked over to Samson and Tango with her hands out. Jorge released their leashes and they trotted up to her, rubbing up against her legs, and pushing their big heads into her hands so she could pet them.

"Wow, they are big lumps of love, aren't they," my mom said.

"Oh, yeah. Samson is still aggressive around most of the male dogs. But, as I said, he's getting better."

"He's missing an ear. Can't say I blame him," Mom replied.

Peggy Kelley called out into the yard. "Hi, Casey."

"Hi, Peggy. This is Mom, Karen Riley."

Peggy Kelley walked out towards us. She shook my mom's hand. "Hi, Karen. We're glad to finally have your daughter here officially."

"Us too, Peggy. Thanks for what you've done with this shelter. The town and the animals really need it," my mom said.

"Well, we certainly need your daughter today. I just got a call from the two other kennel assistants. The bridge they take to get down here is flooded, so they can't make it in until later on and a lot of dogs have to be fed and walked."

I looked at my mom. "Honey, I can't. I have an appointment."

"Oh, come on, Mom. They'll probably flake out anyway."

My mom laughed.

"Possibly, but I still have to call to try and reschedule. I'll be right back." My mom walked to her car to get her phone.

"Peggy, I know you don't have my friend, Anna, on the schedule, but I can call her if you'd like."

"You know, I haven't gotten around to putting her on, but I did plan on it, so yes, by all means."

I got Anna on the phone immediately. She was happy to come as soon as she could get a ride. I was telling Peggy the good news when my mom walked over.

"I can lend a hand as well," she said.

"Wow! That would be fantastic, but not with those shoes. I think there are extra boots in the back."

"I know where they are. Come on, Mom. I'll show you around."

The only boots we could find were hot pink rubber rain boots. I also grabbed a yellow slicker to cover her shirt and trousers.

"I think I'd rather wear these heels," my mom said.

"Mom, we've got over twenty dogs to walk. You'll break an ankle."

"I'll take my chances."

I could hear the dogs howling to be fed and exercised. "Mom, we've got to get going."

"Okay then. But give me your phone," she said.

"My phone? Why?"

"Because you'll end up taking several pictures of my horrendous outfit and it'll end up on Snapchat, Instagram and Facebook."

I reluctantly handed over my phone. "You're cutting off my lifeline."

"Watch what I cut off next if you take a picture."

Since Ron was at a morning rehearsal, I was pretty much on my own until Anna arrived. I know she was pretty bummed that she hadn't been hired yet, but I knew it was only a matter of time. Peggy helped me clean up the kennels while my mom filled all the bowls with fresh dog food and clean water. The dogs needed to walk for a good thirty minutes apiece, so it was going to be a long morning. Fortunately, Anna came by within a half hour.

Anna and I paired up and walked together with the dogs that got along. Mom and Peggy did the same with the others. I was hoping they would have a chance to bond and get to know one another.

By 1:30 we were done exercising all the dogs and took a break on the front porch, waiting for my mom and Peggy to return from their last walk. The sun was drying up the lawn and the two Basset hounds we had with us were lying down in the warm rays. Cleo and Lilly had been tied up to a bench outside the building with a note saying that the family was moving overseas. They thought it would be cruel to quarantine them for three months in a small cage. I understood. That would be tough on these animals that were beyond adorable and loving. Then again, all these dogs were. If I didn't already have Roscoe and Sierra at home, hopefully using their doggie door, I don't know how I'd choose.

I saw my mom and Peggy coming down the hill from the meadow where we would often let the dogs run free. My mom was holding Lulu, a small Cocker Spaniel that still couldn't walk very far.

"Is your mom carrying that dog?" Anna asked.

"Yeah. That's Lulu. Peggy rescued her from a puppy mill the next town up. She couldn't take them all, but wanted to get Lulu out of there. She was kept in a small cage and only being used to mate and breed. She was never let out to exercise."

"That's horrible," Anna said.

"They're called 'brood bitches,' or 'lifers.' They serve a life sentence of having one litter after another until their bodies wear out."

"What happens when they are too old to have puppies?"

The answer was obvious. I thought my silence would lessen the gruesomeness of the system. I was wrong. Anna's eyes started to fill.

"Sorry," I said.

"No, it was a stupid question, and I asked."

"Look, when you see her up close, it is tough. Basically, she can't walk too well because her nipples are so stretched to the ground from nursing. Also she was cooped up in such a small space, her muscles have atrophied. So we've been trying to build up her strength, until we have to carry her. But here's the thing, she couldn't walk at all just last week. Now she can, little by little. She just gets tired quickly."

My mom placed Lulu on the ground. She just lay there. It was heartbreaking, but I knew she would get better. She was still young, and finally in good hands. Then I saw my mom shake Peggy's hand and my imagination started to percolate. They had been walking together for a few hours so I'm sure they got to know one another. More than that, I was hoping the need for a shelter supervisor came up.

"Anna, would you mind taking Cleo and Lilly back in? I just want to talk to my mom about something."

"Sure," Anna said, and led the hounds back inside.

My mom was carrying Lulu while she and Peggy walked towards me up the hill. As they got closer, I could tell they were pretty engaged in a lively conversation.

"Well, it looks as if the dogs will enjoy a nice afternoon outside in the yard," I said.

"Yes, it does," Peggy, said. "And the two volunteers who were rained out earlier should be here any minute, so we'll have plenty of help. But, thanks to you and your mom, the dogs didn't have to wait."

"Glad it all worked out," I said.

Peggy shared a glance with my mom. "In more ways than one. Casey, how would you feel about working here *under* your mom?"

This is exactly what I wanted for her. My mom had been unhappy for so long that this was almost too good to be true. And none of it would have come together if I hadn't been sentenced to work here. Seeing my mom smile the way she was right now made this summer experience beyond worthwhile. It was all meant to be.

"Peggy, this is one time where I'd be happy to be working for my mom."

"Are you sure, honey?" my mom asked. "I mean, Peggy and I would really like to give it a try."

Mom really did have a way with dogs. Every time she spoke, Lulu would lick her face. She didn't flinch and just kept right on talking. That was the first time I'd seen the worn-out Cocker Spaniel show any expression of comfort or love. "I think it's great, and I know you'll be great, Mom."

"I think so too," Peggy said. "We're going to hash out a few things over lunch and be back in a bit. Sound good?"

"Sounds great," I said.

Mom gave me a wink as she and Peggy headed into the office, passing Anna as she came back outside. Seeing my mom's hot colors up close made Anna's eyes open wide as she approached me.

"Whoa! Your mom's outfit is blinding."

"It's pretty ridiculous. But, that lady wearing the hot pink rain boots, neon yellow slicker, oversized hat, and carrying the Cocker Spaniel, is the new shelter supervisor." I couldn't have been prouder.

When Mom and Peggy returned to the shelter after lunch, my mom was beaming. At first, she arranged her shelter schedule to work four days a week, so she could finalize any deals she had with a couple of her buyers. It was amazing how her mood had changed from the morning. "It's funny," Mom said, while we were driving back home later on that day, "Peggy can't pay me much right now, but I don't even care. It's a steady check. Bills will get paid."

"You're going to do great things at that shelter, Mom."

"I have some ideas. I think it's going to help."

"It already has." We were both dirty and sweaty, but my mom looked more relaxed and relieved than I had seen her in months.

It was a good thing because when we walked in the door at 6:15 it was obvious that Roscoe and Sierra had forgotten to wipe their paws. There were wet, muddy skid marks around the entire kitchen and into the laundry room. I held my breath as I followed chunks of dirt out into the hallway toward the living room. I was hoping the trail wouldn't lead me to the sofa and rug. I exhaled when it stopped right by the foyer.

Whew!

I went back outside to where my mom was wiping down Sierra with a wet towel, while Roscoe sat watching. From the way Sierra was groaning with delight, the rub down must have felt like a massage, and Roscoe was looking forward to his turn.

"She took to you quickly, Mom."

"Well, you paved the way. She's a good girl."

"I'll get a mop," I said.

"Oh, honey, don't worry about it. Let it dry and we'll just vacuum it all up. I should have put a big mat down anyway. Next time it rains like that, we'll bring their beds and toys into the kitchen and close the door."

My father came home from work and peeked his head inside the kitchen door. He looked as if he was trying to assess without asking if this was a meltdown moment. I shook my head and he clapped his hands together with relief. "Okay, how 'bout we head over to the *Chart House* for a bite," he said quickly.

Just then, Patty walked in. "Wow, that's quite a mess those dogs made." Thanks for the obvious, Patty.

"Really?" my mom said. "I hadn't noticed."

The day must have melted our brains. I tried to hold it in, but it was no use. I just spit out a bellyful of laughter, which hurled my mother into an episode of hysterics. We couldn't stop. Patty just looked at my dad, who shrugged his shoulders. Sierra got caught up with our crazy high spirits. She jumped up and grabbed the towel that my mother was using to wipe her down. She spun around like a tornado several times, then flew outside the doggy door and down the porch steps. Roscoe just stared at her like she had lost her marbles, then caught the crazy bug as well. They chased each other around the wet yard with the towel trailing behind her like a cape in the wind. Sierra's light gray coat quickly became muddy again. From the width of my mom's smile, she couldn't have cared less.

I t was a little strange that after our almost kiss in his car a couple of weeks ago, Ron and I had seen each other less and less. I was trying to convince myself there was a reason that had nothing to do with me.

*Right?*

*Right.*

Since opening night was at the end of the week, Ron had to spend most of his time at the theater and less time working at the shelter. This fact helped lower the mental alarm of 'where is our relationship going?'

I liked Ron a lot, but he was leaving for college in just a few weeks. I was going to try and follow the advice my mom gave me at the beginning of the summer, to just let things be.

It helped that I was super busy myself. Peggy Kelley and my mom had pretty much completed the staffing needs of the shelter. Mom arranged a visit to the high school with Principal Langdon once school reopened. She planned on talking to an auditorium full of students about opportunities at the shelter for completing their graduate requirements for community service. She also asked Patty if the editor of the *Riverton Press* would be interested in doing a profile on 'The Animal of the Week', so a different picture of a dog or cat, along with their life story, was published on the front page of each edition.

To reach even more people, she invited *River TV*, the town's cable station, to visit the new shelter. A cameraman and producer came and did a report featuring all the adoptable animals, as well as promoting our low cost vet clinic available for neutering, spaying and inoculations. Mom suggested they film me sitting inside the kennels holding a dog or cat while talking about how they came to us and why. It gave a real personal touch for the viewers. That evening the story replayed itself on *River TV* for several hours.

The next day, before nine a.m., a line was forming outside the entrance. Maureen and I were sitting at the reception desk getting ready to field questions from the potential adopters. I had a feeling many were going to need help completing the very thorough adoption application my mom and Peggy had created.

Mom walked over to see if we were ready to open up for the crowd outside.

"Don't you think people will be turned off by this third degree of questioning?" I asked her. "I mean, why do we need their vet's name?"

"Honey, that's the most important question to ask. We have to call the vet to make sure they took care of their animals in the past."

"What if this is their first pet?" I asked.

"Then we need to ask them questions to make sure they know what they are getting involved with. A pet is like a child. This is not about invading their privacy. And if they think that, then they shouldn't be pet owners. It's about assessing their situation to be good animal parents."

For these first time pet owners, my mom created free classes to educate them about proper training, feeding, and the overall best way to raise a healthy dog or cat. "If we eliminate the unknown, people will be less likely to freak out when they see how much time and money it takes to care for a pet." Mom believed this would reduce the number of owner surrenders—which was really high for an affluent town like Riverton.

An hour later, I was signing up one young couple for one of these classes when Ron walked in. "Hey, star," I said.

"Hi, Ron," Maureen said. "We miss you."

"Well, after the last show on Sunday, I'll be back full time."

"Until you leave for school," I said, and then regretted how needy that sounded.

"Well, that's a given, but I think you're calling the wrong person a star. I saw you on *River TV* last night. Your fans are lining up outside the door."

"Well, they're not coming to see me."

"You looked great. I wish I had thought of using the town's channel more," he said.

"I don't think you had much time to think of anything other than keeping the shelter going," I said.

"Really, Ron," Maureen said. "You did an amazing job with what you had to work with. We'll look forward to you coming back next summer." She wasn't the only one.

Just then, my mom walked over, looking a tad serious but trying to sound casual. It seemed a little forced. "Hi, Ron," she said. "Opening night this Friday, right?"

"Yes, Mrs. Riley. Hope you guys can make it."

"Of course we'll be there. Casey, honey, can I talk to you in the back for a minute?"

"Mom, we're kind of busy out here. Can't you just tell me now?"

"It will only take a minute. Ron, you don't mind stepping in for a bit, do you?"

"Okay. I know that look of yours, which is kind of scary. Please just spit it out."

"Okay, well, Alice Bender is here and she would like to bring Roscoe back home."

"What?"

"Remember, it was only a foster in the first place."

"Yeah, but you said we could keep him. In fact, it was your idea." I realized I was getting pretty loud when Ron squeezed my arm.

"I didn't think they could take him back. But now they can. Their situation has changed."

"How?"

"Let's go into my office, honey."

My mom escorted me down the hall as I looked back at Ron. I wish he could have come with me. I really thought the Benders were just delaying the inevitable, and soon Roscoe would officially be part of our family. I couldn't believe this was happening. How the hell could I separate him and Sierra?

Alice Bender was sitting in the chair opposite my mom's desk. This lady was beginning to irritate me.

"Hi, Casey," she said. "Sorry about all this confusion."

"Roscoe is the one that's going to be confused. He's really happy hanging with us."

"I'm sure he is, but you can come over any time you like."

"As long as Dr. Bender isn't around."

"Casey!" Mom said, with emphasis on the second syllable of my name. "I apologize, Alice, for my daughter's incredible rudeness."

"Well, if he didn't like Roscoe, he certainly isn't going to like Sierra," I said.

"Casey, I know you're upset, but you better—" my mom said before Alice interrupted her.

"No, it's okay, Karen. I understand. Look, Casey, he isn't going to be returning for many months. Dr. Bender was arrested on a DWI. Not only did he resist arrest, he punched the officer who pulled him over."

"And I thought doctors were supposed to be smart," I said.

"He's very smart, a little too smart, just not very wise," Mrs. Bender said.

"But he could be coming back, right? I mean, Mom, right now, Maureen and I are interviewing potential adopters and the bar you and Peggy raised was pretty high. I mean, no offense to Mrs. Bender here, but it seems to me you're taking an exception, as well as a risk, by releasing Roscoe back into their home. The dude threatened to kill Roscoe. We're being unfair to those people out there who we're restricting to a higher standard. If Mrs. Bender walked in right now and filled out an application, you know as well I that she wouldn't pass."

My mom looked a little embarrassed, but I could tell she wasn't angry anymore. She gave a big sigh and rolled her chair away from her desk. I guess she needed room to breathe. "She's right, Alice, you wouldn't. But, Casey, this isn't Mrs. Bender and Cindy's fault. They deserve another chance. They rescued Roscoe off the streets and gave him a good safe home for a year. She's not responsible for what her husband threatened to do, and if you remember, Cindy protected him and called the police."

"Yeah, and if you remember, they willingly surrendered Roscoe into our hands, after we set a policy where we weren't taking any more owner surrenders. We did them a favor, and I'm the one who got him out of the shelter, brought him home and found him the love of his life." I knew my mother must have agreed, because as angry as I was getting, she wasn't stopping me. She knew I was right. Besides, this wasn't about my needs, or having a personal vendetta against them. "This is about Roscoe's safety. Nothing else."

"Casey, he'll be safe," Alice said. "I'm so impressed with your passion and honesty, so now let me be honest. Dr. Bender isn't the only one who's been less than wise. I've shown some pretty poor judgment myself. I should never have asked the judge to lift the restraining order. I thought my husband had healed. He hadn't. I was trying to be fair to my family. I should have realized some people can't change, and we just have to let go. The restraining order has been reinstated. I've filed for divorce and Dr. Bender is serving time in jail. When he gets out, if he violates the restraining order again, with his criminal record now, he'll be going away for a very long time. He's not that stupid and neither am I, not anymore. Cindy and I both really miss our dog. Please give us another chance."

I wanted to be fair to Alice and Cindy, but more than that, I wanted to be fair to Roscoe and Sierra. It was pretty clear my mom was putting this decision in my hands and I wasn't too happy with my heightened level of responsibility.

I smacked my hands on my lap and got up from the chair. "All right then, I hope Cindy will let Sierra and Roscoe have some playtime. I think it would be sad to not let them see each other."

"I couldn't agree more and, as I said, we have a huge yard."

"We have a pretty big yard too, Mrs. Bender."

"I didn't mean to imply that ours was somehow—"

"No, I'm sure you didn't." The room was beginning to close in on me and I needed to get out of there. "Cindy can visit us as well. If she'd like."

"I'll tell her. I'm sure she would."

"Okay then," my mom said. "Alice, you just need to fill out an application which, as Casey said, is pretty detailed. I do have to run it by Peggy Kelley, but I'm pretty certain we'll get Roscoe back to you."

"Thank you, Karen. Thank you, Casey."

"Just thank Roscoe for me. As many times a day you can." My throat started to tighten and I realized the dam was going to bust. I made a fast exit, and walked quickly through a throng of potential adopters without making eye contact with Ron and Maureen. I went in the back storage room and bawled my eyes out. I soon felt someone's hands on my shoulder. I didn't need to turn around to know whose they were.

"This sucks," I said.

"I know. I know it does," Ron said as he held me in his arms.


It didn't help when I arrived home later that evening to find Roscoe and Sierra waiting at the front door, tails dusting the floor and tongues hanging out through their smiles. I kneeled in front of them, and with perfect timing, they put their heads on my shoulders. "Did you guys rehearse this?" I looked into his brown, and her blue eyes while scratching them behind the ears. It's as if they were listening closely to what I had to say, almost as if they knew. "Look, this is no big deal. Just no more sleepovers. Okay? I'm going to make sure you get to see each other as much as possible. We'll go on long walks, and swims, and run around in whichever yard happens to be bigger and better. I don't care. As long as you two get to fly around it together. *Comprenden? Bueno.*"

The door opened and my mom walked in. She looked at me for a moment without saying anything, then kneeled down next to me, rubbing Roscoe's ears as Sierra rolled to her back, expecting a belly rub.

"You did the right thing, sweetie."

"I don't know about that, Mom. One thing I do know."

"What's that?"

"I'm not going to be able to take him over there. You can. I realize it's not as if I'm taking him to be euthanized or anything…"

"Oh, God, Casey…"

"Still, I can't let him loose in a yard that's better than ours."

"She didn't say that. Besides, they're going to come by the shelter tomorrow and pick him up."

"So, Peggy approved it?"

"Yes, she did."

"So, that's that then," I said.

My mom kissed me on the forehead, then got up and walked to the kitchen.

"Oh, Mom?"

"Yeah?"

"Can I have tomorrow off?"

I needed to give my swollen eyes a rest and stayed away from the shelter for a few days. I decided instead to help out at the theater. I was expecting her to say 'no way.' Still, I called Anna to see if she wanted to join me. After all, I was there for one reason only, to see Ron. To my surprise, she said yes.

We showed up a few hours before dress rehearsal on Thursday. Joshua Brown, the director, said how unfortunate it was that I had to turn down the role of Rizzo. I told him how I actually ended up having an amazing summer, so it was no huge loss. But my curiosity reared its ugly head and I had to dig, "Besides, I'm sure Sylvia Buchwald has been amazing?"

"Yeah, when she showed up for rehearsals."

"Oh, wow. That's too bad."

"She should be fine tonight. It was just unfair for the other actors. Anyway, thanks for coming in. We could use some help in the makeup department. How are you with applying cosmetics?"

I looked at Anna, with her styled hair and perfectly lined lips and eyes. If I used lip gloss, it was for a special occasion. "Well, as you can see, I'm not too familiar in that area. But I'd be good at changing the set between scenes."

"All I can see is that you're one of those natural girls who doesn't need it."

"Right," I said, feeling a bit of warmth in my cheeks.

Anna shook her head. "Don't listen to her, Joshua. I can show her what to do."

"Cool." He looked at his watch. "So, the guys are in the first scene in an hour. Lots of slicked back hair for them. Then move on to the girls, with lots of red lipstick and hairspray."

"Got it," Anna said.

"I'm going to let the costume stylist know you're here. She'll get you set up in the back."

He left, and Anna turned to me. "Why do you do that?" she asked, rather seriously.

"Do what?"

"You know."

"Well, what would you say to that? 'Aw, shucks, I know, I'm so au naturel. La Dee Da.' He was just being nice because I happen to be standing next to you."

"You don't think you're beautiful?"

"He didn't say that, and no, I would not use the word 'beautiful' to describe me."

"You're nuts, you know that?" Anna said, and walked off shaking her head.

"Now, that I'd agree with," I said, while following behind her.

Since the guys in the show needed less cosmetic attention, I was responsible for getting them all pancaked and powdered. Anna got the girls and, of course, Sylvia Buchwald. God knows where her liner would have ended up if I were the one applying it.

Ron and I were hysterical as I wiped his face with a small wet sponge soaked in liquid foundation.

"Ooh, this feels disgusting. Like a cold, soggy sponge."

"That's because it is a cold, soggy sponge."

"I never had this stuff on my face in any of my shows at school."

"Hey, this is the big time, buddy. Hold still." He grabbed my hand and dabbed my nose with the stuff. "Gee, thanks, I'm sure that looks very attractive."

"Actually, you do look pretty adorable."

"Right." Then, trying to learn from Anna's brief therapy session, I added, "Except for that oil spill on top of your head, you look pretty cute yourself, Kenickie."

I could hear Anna nearby having a tough time with Sylvia Buchwald, who wanted everything just right. "Hey, are you flirting with my boyfriend?" Sylvia asked me, with passive-aggressive seriousness. Ron and I were so caught up in our clowning around that we couldn't respond.

"That's what the hair styles called for back then. It's pretty gross though," he said. "It'll take more than one shampoo to make my hair eco-friendly again."

"Nah, it looks good. Now, for the final touches." I brushed his face with a large puff. That made him sneeze right into the canister of powder, blowing it into my face; that erupted my own series of sneezes. Our ridiculously loud laughing caused everyone to look our way, including Sylvia, who got her answer better than I could have said it myself.

Matt was the last actor I had to prepare for dress rehearsal. I had a feeling Cindy would be sitting on his lap while I applied his makeup, and she was the last person I wanted to be around. After having such a blast with Ron, I didn't want to wreck my mood by being reminded of the whole fiasco with Roscoe. I got that she loved her dog and none of this was her fault, but because of her history, the whole situation really pissed me off.

I went out into the auditorium to look for him. He was sitting on a stool while Cindy painted his face. I tried to be as casual as I could. "You look to be in good hands there, Matt."

"If you say so," he said rather sarcastically.

Cindy was attempting to put powder on his face and he almost smacked her hand away. "Damn girl, you got stuff in my eyes."

"Sorry, you keep moving," she said.

"Let Casey take over here," Ron said.

Talk about feeling uncomfortable. Cindy looked up at me with pleading eyes— which I couldn't tell if she meant 'please take over for me' or 'please go away so I can prove myself to him.'

"Hey, I just finished with Ron and he's still sneezing the dust out of his nose."

"No, really, I'm not very good at this," Cindy said, and with that, she got up to leave. "Break a leg, babe." Cindy leaned over to give Matt a kiss on the cheek.

He pulled away from her like she was contagious. "Watch the makeup."

This was a side of Matt I had never seen before. As she walked away, we both gave each other an expression of support. I sat down next to Matt and saw that nothing really needed to be added. "You look pretty much done to me. "

"You're kidding," he said. "I must look like a friggin' ghost. She didn't even put any of that red stuff on my cheeks yet."

Was this guy for real? I never knew him that well, but he'd always seemed incredibly charming, maybe a little too charming. There must have been a reason why Anna stayed clear. Now I see it wasn't just her fear of Cindy, though that was reason enough.

"Actually, this is above my pay grade, Matt. I'm going to grab the head costume stylist. I heard she's worked on Broadway," I lied.

"Awesome," he said, while gawking at himself in the mirror.

And he believed me. I made my escape, until Cindy called out.

"Casey, wait up." She walked toward me, out of Matt's earshot. "Thought you might want to hear that Roscoe is doing good."

"He's a good dog." I turned away again.

"Maybe I could swing by sometime and he and Sierra could have a play date."

There was a part of me that wanted to play tough and tell her I'd get back to her with an air of 'hell no.' But that wouldn't have been good for the dogs or Cindy, or me, for that matter.

"She'd love it." I started to walk off, then turned back around. I peered over her shoulder in Matt's direction. He was too busy admiring himself in the mirror to care about us. "And how are you doing?"

"Not bad for a kid whose father is in the slammer." She noticed when I looked over at Matt. "My boyfriend is not like my father."

"No, of course not. It's not that. I just never would have taken the leather, bike and tough guy appearance for someone who is um, you know…"

"… a prima donna." For the first time the two of us shared a good laugh at the crazy irony of the whole thing. If anything, Ron, with his prep school background and ivy-league school intentions, should have played the part of Narcissus. But here was Matt, giving the academy-award-winning performance.

"Give me a call anytime," I said, still laughing.

"Thanks," Cindy said.

"Thank the dogs."

I made my way back stage and found Anna still working on Sylvia's face. She gave me a look of complete misery.

"All righty then. Looking good, Sylvia. Anna, why don't we grab some lunch."

"Oh, no, not yet," Sylvia whined. "Can you put more foundation under my eyes? I didn't sleep very well last night. Nerves."

"Sylvia, no one in the audience is going to see your bags up on stage."

"I have bags?"

"Well, you think you do."

"Then so will Ron, or rather Kenickie."

"He couldn't care less," I said.

"How do you know?" she asked.

"She knows," Ron said, as he walked through the back stage door.

Barring a few minor glitches with the lights and the props, the dress rehearsal went smoothly. Opening night was even better. Not only could Ron sing like a Broadway star, he was also a great dancer, and took the choreography to a different level.

When the supporting cast came out on stage the applause was loud. Then Ron came out holding Sylvia's hand and half the audience stood up clapping. Matt made the final bow with the actress playing Sandy. Her Army Ranger boyfriend was sitting near me, and he completed the standing ovation, yelling out, "Bravo!"

The director walked two bouquets of flowers out on stage. Matt took one and handed it to Sandy. Ron took the other and handed it to Sylvia. Then he picked out one flower from the bunch and walked down into the audience. I wasn't quite sure what he was doing, or where he was headed, until he walked right up to me and handed me the flower with a kiss on my cheek. I felt amazing. I felt even more so when Matt duplicated Ron's gesture and did the same for Cindy. Though she was sitting three rows away, she held up her rose and we toasted each other, warming the cold distance between us.

The summer came to a close. Junior year would start for me, and freshman year at Cornell would soon start for Ron. We didn't get all serious about what was going to happen when he left for school. We didn't need to. We were really good friends, nothing more. Months ago, my mom told me to try and let things be and not try and fix everything. I really didn't get what she meant back then, but now I was living it, and it had a way of making things so much easier. Maybe that's why things were so easy with Ron. I don't know. I didn't care because it was working. I wasn't going to lie to myself though. I mean, if he came back over Thanksgiving with a hot girlfriend in tow, I would be pretty bummed, and yes, I'll admit it, jealous. But having a fear of that happening, or attaching myself to him to try and prevent it, was useless. Still, I couldn't help but wonder where the shelter (code word for me) fit in with his holiday schedule. I knew he was committed to helping out the animals whenever he could. I just wasn't sure how committed he was to me.

"What about spring break?" I asked him, after we closed up for the night. It was his last day of work before he took off for college, and for the first time ever we were walking the border of where our relationship began and ended. Summer was still thick in the air, and though a hint of fall was nowhere to be felt in the humid stillness, it was upon us.

"What about it?" he said.

"Aren't you going to hit the beach down in Florida, like most college students? You can't work all the time. Everyone needs a little vacation."

"Working with you is like a vacation."

"Shut up. That's so lame." I knew he was only half serious about that, but it did feel good hearing it. We did have a good time together and I was going to miss him.

"My family usually goes skiing out west in March. I have two weeks off, so I might do a little of that, and then put some time in here. It's hard for me to stay away from the animals for too long. I like to check in."

Was I included in that category? Let it go, I was telling myself. "What about near Cornell? I'm sure those shelters have a need for people like you."

"Big time. I already made plans to work in the Clinton Town Shelter one day a week, and let me tell you, the dogs here have it great."

"I don't think I could work any place where the dogs are kept in bad conditions."

"Then you wouldn't work in any other facility, because this is like a resort hotel."

"I don't want to think about it."

"No, you don't. I also have a week off at Thanksgiving, so I'll be here a couple of days as well. I know holidays are really tough on animals in questionable situations. That's usually the time they get dumped or … even worse. Peggy is going to need an extra hand, so I'm glad to do it. So when does school start for you?"

"A week from today."

"Junior year. You're getting up there, Casey."

"It's so weird. Soon, I'll have to start thinking about colleges."

"Any idea where you'd like to start looking."

"Most likely a state school. I don't want to burden my parents with that kind of tuition. That's just crazy. Patty wasn't able to go to Princeton, so it wouldn't be fair if I got my first choice. Then again, my sister can be a pain in the butt, and we've have had some angry fights. Still, she's always wanted the best for me. My father's agency is also doing much better, and my mom isn't relying on commission anymore, so who knows?"

"Any idea what you want to study?"

"Before the summer, I wanted to be a writer. In fact, tomorrow I'm stopping by to see my old English teacher. I was supposed to show him some samples I'd done over the last few months. Then I got caught up with other things. Now I seem to have made a one-eighty degree turn in my thinking. I'm actually moving away from the arts now and leaning toward the sciences."

"You want to be a vet."

"I do. I just don't know if I could handle the emotional trauma. The other day, my father didn't know that Sierra was sleeping underneath the kitchen table. When he moved his chair out, he pinched her tail. She made this high-pitched yelp that stopped my heart. My father was more upset about what it did to me than to her. She was fine. I was a mess, and cuddled with her on the floor until my heart slowed down."

"They say the same about doctors. They can be brilliant and calm when it comes to their patients, but if a family member gets hurt, they freeze. I think you'd be amazing. You know, Cornell has one of the best vet schools in the country."

"Really?"

The following morning, I rode my bike down the rough lane toward Mr. Davis' house. He liked the fact that it wasn't paved. "Keeps out those who can't handle a few bumps in the road," he told me once. He and his wife Sarah lived on the top of a hill that overlooked the Hudson. It reminded me of a tree house. They had this huge cedar porch that wrapped around a rustic wood-framed, chalet-style cabin. They had one son who was away at Medical school down south. When I walked inside, the doors and windows on either side of the home were open and the ceiling fans in full swing. It was a beautiful day and the breeze through the house felt awesome.

Mr. Davis greeted me at the front door. He was wearing a light plaid shirt, rolled up at the sleeves, and a pair of work pants. He was holding his reading glasses in one hand and a mug of coffee in the other. Even though he was sporting a two-day, five o'clock shadow, his eyes were bright, and he looked more rested than I had seen him these last two years. I heard the familiar sound of paws scraping the wood floor. His two labs raced around the corner to welcome me, one black, the other almost white in color.

"Oh my God. They are gorgeous. What are their names?"

"Scout and Jem."

"That's great," I said, while scratching them behind the ears. A loyal brother and sister. "Do they have a father, Atticus? Named after the first book, of course, not the second."

"Maybe. There's always room in my heart and home for another dog."

"Our heart, maybe, but not our home." Sarah Davis came into the room, holding two leashes. She had a very small frame, but appeared fit and strong. Her salt and pepper hair was cut short, and she wore a denim shirt with loose chinos. She had on a pair of worn leather hiking shoes. "Hi, you must be Casey Riley."

"Yes, Mrs. Davis, nice to meet you. Love your home, and these dogs are beautiful. Where'd you get them?"

"Call me Sarah." At first glance, one might think Sarah Davis was a bit cold, very dry and direct in her delivery, but she had a way of smiling through her blue eyes without moving her mouth. "They actually never graduated from Seeing Eye school."

"No way," I said. "These guys?"

"I know. Their failure was our good fortune."

"I'd say."

"Jem here has a heart condition, so we can't let him run around as much as we'd like. So we walk him on the leash as often as possible. Scout here runs around more than her brother and gets into all sorts of trouble," Mr. D. said.

"Just like Harper Lee's character," I said.

"And they came up from Alabama."

"Did you read Lee's second novel?" I asked, referring to *Go Set a Watchman*.

"Actually, it was her first, published long after *To Kill a Mockingbird*. I haven't yet, but I plan on it. My wife has."

"Yes, just finished it. It is a completely separate story, set in a different time. The name, Atticus is the same. The character is not. That is all I will say about it."

"Speaking of stories, you have one to show me?" Mr. D. asked.

"Actually, Scout and Jem aren't the only ones who failed here."

Sarah headed out the door, holding both dogs on their leashes. "Well, I'll be back in about an hour. Casey, how about staying for lunch? We have salad from the garden and homemade bread."

"Sounds great, Mrs. ... I mean, Sarah."

I followed Mr. D. outside and sat next to him in one of the Adirondack chairs looking out over the hill. He started filling up a pipe with sweet-smelling tobacco. "Sarah doesn't like it when I smoke inside the house."

"From the looks of your wife, I would say she doesn't like it when you smoke at all."

"You are correct. As long as I keep it to two a day, she doesn't say anything."

"And do you?"

"I try."

"I'm sure that's good enough for her, Mr. D."

"It is. Is it good enough for you?"

"You're speaking of my attempt at writing?"

"I am."

"I don't think I got that far. I don't even think I tried."

"I find that hard to believe," he said, while letting out a plume of smoke that he savored. No one in my family smoked. The idea of being close to such a carcinogen was not something I ever thought I would like. But out here on the deck, with the scent of pine and the river nearby, it smelled like it belonged. It felt okay, natural almost.

"I don't think I turned on my computer once this summer."

"But you experienced the summer, right?"

"That I did. It was the best summer I ever had. Come to think of it, I did give my sister an idea to expand her article on the Riverton Family Retreat. But that's about as far as I got."

"That's the women's shelter downtown?"

"Yep."

"And you worked for the animal shelter all summer long."

"That's right."

"Creativity comes from our experiences, Casey. You know that. "

"I do, but now I'm thinking I might be able to make more of a difference doing something else."

"And what were you thinking?"

"I was thinking about being a vet."

"And why couldn't you do both?"

"I don't know. They just seem like opposites. One is scientific, and well, one is artistic."

"Did you ever hear of the writer, James Herriot?"

"I think so. Yeah, I have. I forgot about him."

"There are a few of his books in the back study. They're yours. Give yourself some time and then, when you feel like it, write about something that moved you over the summer. Something important to you. With your sister's help, you might even be able to get it published in the *Riverton Free Press*."

"But that's reporting, not really creative writing."

"How do you think Steinbeck and Hemingway got their start?"

"They were reporters?"

"Yes. Very good ones."

"I think I already have an idea, Mr. D."

"Of course you do."

"Funny, in the back of my mind, I felt guilty all summer long about not putting any time aside to write. Now, I realize, I was trying all along, but I didn't even know it."

"That's the best kind."

Two and a half months flew by. I had no sooner started my junior year when I was in the store with my mom ordering our free-range organic, twenty-pound turkey. I had talked to my sister's summer boss, the editor of the *Riverton Free Press*, to pitch an idea. He liked it and said it would be perfect for the holidays. I had been working on it but ran into a snag. I didn't want to hit people over the head with what I was trying to get across, but at the same time, it was missing something. I talked to Mr. D and he said to let it sit, that I had time, and it would come to me. It was a good thing, because my life had been busier than ever.

My part-time gig at the shelter kept me hopping. My mom wanted me to take a break and 'Be a normal teenager.'

"Why start now?" I said.

"Don't be fresh," she replied.

I tried staying away for a few days and missed the animals too much. Plus, there was never a shortage of things for me to do there. It was also really easy to bring Sierra over and let her play with the dogs. Cindy had texted me a few times to meet up at her house and, as much as I wanted to, I just couldn't make it happen. I suggested we meet at the shelter. She probably assumed Anna would be there and never took me up on it. Anna had long gotten over the Saturday sabotage. I think Cindy not only felt bad about it, but was also seriously embarrassed by the whole dark event. I had seen a change in her the few times I bumped into her at school. She seemed less angry at the world, almost friendly. Even though it was a bitter pill for a kid to swallow, maybe her dad being in jail was the best thing for her family. God only knows how long he had been tormenting her and her mom. Probably as long as Cindy had been tormenting other kids. Damn vicious circle. I wanted to trust her more and felt that maybe if I showed her that I did, it would help in some small way. I told her I would have a little more time over Thanksgiving weekend and I would swing by then. She said she'd be around, and Roscoe would really like that. I knew "Roscoe" included her as well, but she wasn't able to say it. I understood. I was still a little wary of getting too friendly myself.

My time at the shelter wasn't work. It was a blast. Mom had expanded it beyond just being a facility for sheltering dogs, but also for rehabilitating the ones who needed it. She also used it as a foundation for reaching out to the community, and other area shelters, to promote responsible and loving dog ownership. She had the paper, and the local cable, and radio station run her campaign that encouraged rescuing a dog over buying one through pet shops and puppy mills.

"Look," she told the Ad Directors, "I don't want to put anyone out of business. There's a small market place for breeding if it's done ethically. But why the hell would anyone spend one thousand on a dog when there are so many homeless animals and lovable dogs being gassed due to overcrowding and underfunded shelters?"

She got them to run print ads, web ads and radio spots all pro-bono. She also created T-Shirts and sweatshirts with the logo "Save a Life—Adopt an Animal" and sold them at the shelter. I organized adopt-a-thons at George Washington High for people to come and see first-hand how awesome these animals were. We moved dogs and cats to great homes at such speed that high-kill shelters out of state contacted us to take their animals out of harm's way. My mom loved her job. She usually worked six days a week and I had never seen her happier.

For the last few months, Ron and I had kept in touch through a few emails, but mostly texts and a few Facebook posts. The good thing about being so busy was I had less time to stalk him, and see where his social life had taken him. I was curious, of course, but afraid to look. I knew he had arrived home the Saturday before Thanksgiving, so I was surprised to hear he hadn't come by the shelter. I tried to convince myself it didn't really matter. I had a few exams that week, so I wasn't there anyway.

Thanksgiving we were closed to the public, but Anna and I showed up in the morning to take the dogs out in the yard, and walk the ones who weren't ready for full socialization. I was returning from my hike down the hill with Tango and Samson. Samson was doing so much better. Jorge had done an amazing job. When he was there, it was fine to let Samson out with the other dogs in the yard. But since Jorge was out in L.A. spending time with his family, it was a good idea to take Samson out separately with a dog we knew he was comfortable with. It was only a matter of time before he felt safe being around all of them. Seeing the nasty scar where his ear had been made me realize how forgiving these dogs were. If I was missing an ear due to a vicious fight, I don't think I'd ever trust again. As it was, I didn't fully trust Cindy and I was still trying to get over that.

Tango sensed him first. She pulled so quickly on her leash that I lost hold of it. I turned around and Ron was on the ground with her on top of him. I let Samson go and he joined in the wrestle.

"Don't you know better than to sneak up on a girl when she's protected by two eighty-pound pit bulls?"

Ron had slobber all over his jeans. The two lumps of love were hugging him with their bodies. "Some protection. They're licking me to death."

"Better them than me."

"Whoa! Miss Riley. I'm not quite sure how to take that."

"You know, I'm not even quite sure why I said that."

"Nerves, perhaps?"

"Perhaps. You look thinner."

"Well, that's freshman year for ya. You either gain ten or lose ten. I was kinda burning the candle at both ends. Between school and work, I sometimes forgot to eat."

Ron was already a pretty thin guy, and had more of a coffee house, play the guitar and recite-a-poem-type physique than a Matt Barkley build. "It's not as if you could afford that, Ron?"

"That's what my mom said. The last month has been really busy. I've been serving as a liaison between the Clinton animal shelter and the university. I've actually found some great homes for these animals through the students. It's been really successful. I was able to get the administration to allow the animals in the dorms, until the students could take them home for good at Thanksgiving."

"I hope the parents know."

"They had to sign off on it before we could release the animals."

"That's great."

"Well, I saw Peggy yesterday, when I arrived home. She told me your mom is doing similar things with good results."

"You got home just yesterday?"

"Yeah, I was needed at the Clinton shelter for a few days before Thanksgiving. You know how crazy it gets around the holidays, with people dumping their animals, cleaning house and trying to lower their bills any way they can. I thought I told you that."

"That's right, you did. Sorry, I've been crazy busy myself." When Ron texted me about his ETA, I thought he meant he'd be working at our shelter. I felt immediate relief, knowing he hadn't blown me off. Good thing I'd 'let things be' and not tried to fix something that didn't need fixing. Whew! Saved again by my mom's random life lesson statements.

"So, what time is your family feasting out?" he asked.

"Whenever we get back from taking care of these animals. Anna and my mom are in the yard now. After we eat, I'm heading over to Cindy's to let Sierra and Roscoe have a little post meal romp. They haven't been together since the summer. I wonder if they'll remember each other?"

"Oh, you can bet on it. You know what they say about distance and the heart."

"I do. I just didn't think it applied to canines."

"It applies to everybody."

"Dude, are you flirting with me?"

"I believe I am."

"Well, stop. I'm not good at being on the receiving end and it's making me nervous."

"What can I do to not make you nervous?"

"Okay, now you're really making me nervous."

"Well, look, I'm going to hang with my family most of the day, but how 'bout I swing by your place later this evening? I can even pick you up at Cindy's and bring you back to my house. You can meet my folks and two brothers. Cool?"

"Cool." Did he just ask me over to his house to meet his family? Okay, it is Thanksgiving. We are friends. So chill, Casey, don't read anything else into it.

Ron grabbed Samson's leash and we walked down the hill toward the shelter. It wasn't warm and there wasn't a sunset, like our first walk together just a few months ago. It was chilly and a light snow was beginning to fall. Still, it was just as beautiful. We didn't have Shiloh and Sierra. We had Samson and Tango. Four dogs that had recovered from some past pain and moved beyond it into new lives, one of which was mine. The shelter made that happen and this walk, like the other walk before it, was something I would never forget.

Thanksgiving dinner was as it should be: a mix of some family tension, overindulgence, fun, sadness, and what can I say, sympathy for others, and gratitude for us. Patty had arrived that morning. She had spent a few days with her new boyfriend's family over in Nyack. It was her last year at University and she had already nailed a paid internship at the *New York Times*, to start after graduation. She was really excited about living up around Columbia with a few friends in a two-bedroom railroad apartment for around one thousand dollars a month. My father didn't like that idea one bit, and thought it crazy when she could easily live at home rent-free and commute. My mom disagreed and said that everyone young should have a chance to live in the city. "Yeah," my dad said, "as long as they aren't on a strict diet of dried Ramen noodles and PB and Js." My mom and Patty made the same sour face, and then thankfully the doorbell rang.

Anna came with her mom, Jane, who was scheduled to work at the hospital from three to midnight. She was able to switch her shift with someone who needed the overtime more than she did. Sorry for them, happy for Anna. It was the first Thanksgiving without Mr. Swenson, and after a glass of wine, Jane started tearing up. My mother, forever the softie, gave her a big hug, and then Sierra left my feet, from underneath the table, and put her big snout on my mom's shoulder and one paw on Jane's knee. My dad poured another round to toast a man who obviously did a great job helping to raise an even greater daughter. This, of course, made Anna start to cry. Poor Sierra was torn, but decided to switch places and hop up on Annie's lap. She was way too big for that stunt. After placing her two front legs up on Anna's knees, Sierra tried to lift her hind legs up as well. It wasn't happening, until Anna helped her by raising her rear end, and then held her like a big lap dog. Between the laughs and the tears, Sierra was one confused animal, and didn't know whom to comfort next. *Welcome to my crazy family, sweet girl.* She joined in the celebration by howling like the beautiful wolf-dog she was, and licking the tears of joy and grief off Anna's face.

All went pretty smoothly with Anna, Patty and me cleaning up the kitchen, until my sister didn't like Sierra's method of rinsing the plates.

"That's disgusting, Casey," she said.

"You kidding? Dogs have cleaner mouths than people."

"Maybe your mouth," she said.

"Relax, it's going in the dishwasher."

"Dishwasher? We should incinerate them."

"You're getting way too OCD in your old age."

"And you're beginning to sprout oats."

"Oats?" I looked at Anna with a puzzled expression.

"Granola girl," Anna clarified.

"Oh! I'll take that as a compliment. I like granola bars."

"You made my point," my sister said.

"Always happy to help." Patty walked out of the kitchen, shaking her head. "Happy Thanksgiving," I called out.

"And I always regretted being an only child," Anna said.

"That was nothing. Besides, it's the holidays. It usually comes with the territory. Oh, speaking of being an only child. I told Cindy I would go over there to let Sierra and Roscoe run around for a little bit. You want to come?"

"I don't think that would make Cindy too comfortable."

"I'll text her and see what she says. How's that?"

Anna went outside to the living room to watch *It's a Wonderful Life* with Jimmy Stewart and Donna Reed. It was my dad's favorite holiday movie. "My mom's too," Anna said.

Cindy got back to me pretty quickly. She said they would love the company. Because of everything that had happened over the past year, they wanted to keep a low profile and not hang with family. It was just she and her mom, and Roscoe, of course. Her dad had been released yesterday and was spending Thanksgiving with his brother and sister-in-law up in Cold Spring. It made her feel pretty sad, but relieved that he wasn't alone.

I walked out into the living room and my family and friends were a comforting sight. And Sierra? Sierra was lying up on the couch, with her big head in my sister's lap, drooling his toxic saliva all over her two hundred dollar 7 jeans.

"Mom, Dad? Anna and I are going to head over to Cindy's for a bit."

"Now, honey? You'll miss the movie," my mom said.

"Mom, I could recite every line in that movie."

"So could your dad, but that's not stopping him," my mom said. "Need a ride, or are you walking?"

"I think we could both use a walk." And on 'walk,' Sierra jumped off the couch and grabbed the leash in her mouth.

It was an amazing evening, cool and dry. I could smell the smoke from fireplaces going in the neighborhood, and Sierra, for some strange reason, was pulling on her leash. It was almost as if she knew we were heading over to see Roscoe. Strange, considering she'd never been there before. We turned the corner and headed away from the newer development, where my parents lived, to the older neighborhood of wider streets and large stone homes. The Benders lived at the end of a wooded cul-de-sac with tall pine trees and a view of the river. We rang the bell and immediately heard Roscoe barking which, of course, made Sierra start to howl and whine. Alice opened the door and Roscoe flew outside. The two of them jumped on each other while making that playful high-pitched cry of joy. "Oh, my goodness," Alice said. "Happy Thanksgiving. What a reunion." Then they started racing around the front yard and rolling on the ground, with Sierra jumping over Roscoe like a gazelle. "Come on in. Cindy just took her homemade apple pie out of the oven."

"And homemade ice cream," Cindy called out from the kitchen.

"Oh, wow, glad we made room for dessert," I said.

"Let me just get the dogs inside. The backyard is fenced in, but not the front yet."

"Sierra. Come on, girl," Funny, I never trained her, but she certainly knew her name and never hesitated when I called. She jumped up and ran to my side. Roscoe, of course, followed.

The dogs chased each other over the rich-colored Bokhara rugs and around the antique furnishings. I expected Alice to immediately open up the French doors into their football field of a yard. She couldn't have cared less as Roscoe and Sierra ran through a house that could have made the front cover of *Architectural Digest*.

It was beginning to get dark and she turned on the floodlights in the back so we could see them once they went outside.

Cindy greeted us with two plates of pie a la mode. "Thanks for coming by, you guys. I think Roscoe missed Sierra big time."

I took one look at the ice cream, then up at Anna. The two of us caught each other's eye and burst out laughing. "Uh, oh, inside joke apparently," Cindy said.

Anna took her plate and sat down at the kitchen table, trying to soften her laughs, but it was no good. Then I spilled the beans. "The good news is you can laugh about it now, right, Anna?"

"Laugh about what?" Cindy asked.

"Well, to extinguish that fire in my throat, I ate a quart of ice cream, which was why I got sick, which is ..."

"... why you couldn't audition," Cindy added.

"Yes, sireee, Bob. I don't think I've had any since," Anna said, while taking a huge bite of pie with a dollop of ice cream on top.

"Why would you do that?" Alice Bender asked.

"You see, Mom ..."

"... it's a long unimportant story," Anna said, "involving a guy."

"Yeah, a pretty unimportant guy," Cindy said.

"This doesn't involve Matt, does it?" Alice Bender asked.

"Yeah, Mom, it does. But that's all over now."

"What's all over?" I asked.

"Matt and I," Cindy said. "I broke it off yesterday."

"You did? Wow." I didn't mean to sound so surprised, but I was.

"I know, most people are pretty shocked that I was the one who ended it, but the truth is, it shouldn't have gone on as long as it did."

"Well, he treated you pretty horribly, honey," Alice Bender said.

"I treated him pretty poorly, as well, Mom. I treated a lot of people poorly, and for that, I'm really sorry."

"It's okay, Cindy. Your pie and ice cream make up for a lot," Anna said.

"Yeah, and I'm going to eat mine before the good stuff melts." I sat down at the kitchen table while Cindy and her mom got their plates and joined us.


We all talked about school and guys and what we wanted to be when we had to eventually work for a living. Alice asked Anna and me if we drank coffee or cappuccino. We gave two thumbs up to the frothy stuff, then put on our coats and went outside, holding our mugs to watch the dogs play in the yard while Alice went upstairs to check on a few of her listings. There was a full moon and even though it was November it wasn't cold. It was really peaceful outside. An owl started hooting, and we walked through the pine trees down to the river with our two dogs sniffing at the smells all around them.

The floodlights from their yard, and the bright moon, helped us see clearly. The stars and the lights over the Tappan Zee, and from the homes on the other side of the river, were an amazing view.

"As much as I miss the city, I really have come to love it up here. It kind of has a city feel without the dirt and loud traffic," Anna said.

"It's 'stimulating without being oppressive,' is what my dad always says."

"I get that," Cindy said. "But like the city, people are constantly competing against each other, and that I find oppressive."

Considering Cindy had been the one fostering that negative atmosphere, her remark was pretty strange. Maybe she finally realized it and this was her way of letting go. "But we do that to ourselves, don't we? It doesn't have to be that way," I said.

"Yeah, but if you need to make a living and everyone around you is pushing and pushing, how do you stand out, how do you stay in the game?" Cindy asked.

"Maybe we should just play to enjoy it and not play to win all the time. I guess you have to trust that what you're doing is enough for you and not worry about other people," I said.

"But you have to worry about other people," Anna said. "That's what happened to my dad. He was a trader on Wall Street, doing really well. And then suffered a heart attack at the age of forty-eight. It wasn't enough for him to just do what he felt was right, to provide for us, to pay bills. He had to play to win, most times on terms he didn't agree with. And then the market crashed and it wasn't about winning anymore, but just staying in the game. Work was even harder after that. I think it's what killed him." Roscoe trotted over, sat down, and gave Anna his attention. Canines have a way of sensing when someone needs a paw. Sierra, on the other hand, was looking off in the direction of the Bender's house. Her ears and nose were twitching like crazy. Still, she just sat there, assessing, waiting.

"You must miss him very much," Cindy said.

"Every day. You must miss your dad too, though?"

"I do. The way he used to be. But not really now."

Sierra started growling and the hair on her back was up.

"What's up with your dog?" Cindy asked.

"Probably smells a raccoon or something," I said.

"You should put her on a leash. There are coywolves around here." Cindy said.

"What the heck is a coywolf?" Anna asked.

"Hybrid between a coyote and a wolf," Cindy explained.

"That is so cool." I took out my leash and started to walk over to Sierra.

"Maybe your dad will get back to the way he used to be," I said.

And that's when we heard it, that scream of fright. Long after Sierra had sensed something was not right. Before I could clasp the leash to her collar, she bolted toward the Bender's house. Roscoe took off after her and I all I could think about was my dog. Nothing else mattered.

I ran.

As I got closer to the house, the yelling became louder. The neighbors must have heard this. The police would be here soon. Damn, Sierra was fast, and Roscoe was close behind her. It would be okay. There was no way for her to get in. Wait, was there a doggie door? Would Sierra know where it was? No, but Roscoe sure would. I saw Sierra on the deck jumping up on the glass door, trying to get in. Please don't break. I turned around and saw Cindy running up the hill while screaming through the trees. "My mom. Oh, God, please Mom. Dad, no!" Anna was close behind.

Roscoe caught up with Sierra and he disappeared through a side door. I had to get to her before she followed. I tripped going up the porch steps and reached for her mane of fur, but she slipped through my hands. My throat was raw as I yelled for her to stop. Louder and louder, I commanded with the little air left in my lungs. She had always listened to me before. Not now. Her protective instincts took flight. When this mess was over, obedience training was the priority. Then again, I don't think you could train the hero out of any dog.

I threw open the glass door and saw Alice Bender running out the front door, followed by a tall, stocky man. Roscoe was close behind. I followed them around the corner of the house to the breezeway by the garage. I didn't see Sierra. Maybe she got lost in the house. But Alice Bender was on the ground with Dr. Bender on top of her. He had one hand around her neck. The other, the same one he used to perform countless surgeries, was clenched in a fist and raised high above her face.

Roscoe jumped on the doctor's back, but he didn't last for long. An angry punch landed right in Roscoe's side, throwing the forty-pound dog into a stone column, laying him flat. My instincts drew me to his limp body, and then something made me turn. Even when she first came to the shelter, Ron had warned me of Sierra's potential, but I had never seen the teeth she was showing now. She lunged in the air and wrapped her jaw around Bender's hand, the one guarding his throat. He screamed and fell off of Alice onto the driveway, with Sierra in full attack. Out of the corner of my eye, I saw a blur of blue. I turned and saw two police officers. I was too far away. My legs felt like they were in quicksand. Move, I told them. Move. I saw where the gun was pointed. I flew, I heard the shot and felt a hard sharp object pierce my thigh. I grabbed my dog and held her tightly as I rolled my body on top of her. She wasn't getting away from me this time.

I heard my mom, then my dad talking to my mom. I made out Patty's voice. Who was she talking to? Was that Ron? I opened my eyes. My mom's face was red and swollen, but smiling with love and relief.

"Mom. Mom," was all I could say. I felt heavy, but light at the same time. Like I was floating. Then I remembered. "Sierra. Where's Sierra?" I couldn't get up. I was freaking out. Where was my dog? Was my dog all right?

"Sierra is fine, sweetheart," my mom said.

"Where is she?"

"She's at the shelter, our shelter."

"Why? Why isn't she here, or at home? Mom, you've got to bring her home. I don't trust anybody."

Ron came into my view. "Hey, there. I'm going over right now. I'll be with her all day until they release her."

"What do you mean, 'release her?'" I asked him.

"She's just under observation," my dad said. "The police want to make sure she's safe to bring home. It is just a formality."

My family was all around me, but I felt this powerful sense of worry, like I had never felt before. I was defenseless. I wanted out of there. I wanted to see and hold Sierra. I wanted to protect her, like she had protected all of us against that dangerous man. It wasn't fair. "He's unsafe, but he's free. She's safe and back in a cage. It's not right. It's not …" I felt a sting in my arm. My mind emptied. Sleep came.

The doctor said the bullet barely missed my femoral artery. If that vein takes a hit, your blood can drain before they roll you into the ER. The bullet went straight through my leg, without hitting any bone. Yes, I was lucky. And so was Roscoe. He took a nasty blow to the head, and was pretty unsteady for a few days, but after a thorough examination, the vet said he would have a full recovery. And Sierra? Sierra spent a few days in "lock up" at the shelter, but only during the day. My mom snuck her out at night and let her into my bed, only to bring her back before it opened.

My mom got a call from the Animal Control Supervisor, Jack Simmons. He told her this would all be over in a few days and, as far as he was concerned, he was only sorry that Dr. Bender got his hand in the way of his throat. I laughed at that. My mom didn't think it was funny. As appointed by the town, Sierra had a vet and trainer examine her while she was in the pen to assess whether she was harmless to others. She was the sweet dog to everyone who interacted with her. Her only issues had to do with wife and dog beaters. She just wasn't very fond of them.

I graduated from two crutches, to one crutch, to a cane. The stiches came out after about a week, but my mom and dad wanted no part of me going back to school just yet. I didn't mind. I was able to study at home with my dog at my feet. Anna came by almost every day. Cindy came by with Roscoe a few times as well. They ran around the yard, looking as if nothing bad ever happened. That's all I cared about. I would have a small scar on my leg, reminding me how strong the love of friendship can be, and how strong it can make you.

Being at home also helped me finish the story I never seemed to have the time, nor the motivation, to start. After it appeared in the *Riverton Free Press*, the phone rang. My mom picked up and handed it over to me. It was Mr. Davis.

"It's a start, Casey."

I knew what he was talking about. "The only thing, Mr. D., I went through a lot to have those thousand words come out of me. A novel could kill me."

"It doesn't take a tortured soul to be a good writer. Everyone will suffer at some point. Sometimes people like Cindy and Anna experience it at an earlier age than most. It won't be the first time, I'm sorry to say."

"You think it makes you a better writer?" I asked.

"No. There are a lot of people who suffer and can't write. They just can't seem to translate that honesty down on paper. What you have is a passion to get your message out anyway you can. Before, you did it mostly physically, and now you've taken your first step to do it creatively. Don't let it be your last."

"I thought my king snake idea was pretty creative."

"Great. Next time, instead of getting arrested for it, how about getting published? Put your strategy into words. You'd be surprised how interesting it can be."

"I will. Thanks, Mr. D."

"How's the leg?"

"Getting better all the time."

"Good. When it's fully healed, why don't you and Sierra come on over? Scout and Jem would like to meet her."

"Will do."

I hung up the phone when the doorbell rang. Sierra jumped off the couch and ran over. My mom opened it and in walked Ron.

"Hey, you got back early," I said, while giving him a hug.

"My grades were high enough that I didn't have to take any finals."

"Just say it, man. You got all A's."

"I thought I did." Ron stepped back to take a better look at me. "Hey, you aren't limping anymore."

"Finally, it's been four weeks."

"You did take a bullet in the thigh."

"You don't have to remind me." I hadn't told Ron about my editorial, but I'm sure he heard about it. He was glancing at the paper on the coffee table.

"Is that it?" he asked.

"Is that what?"

"Honey, don't play games. Let him read it," my mom said. Picking it up off the table, she handed it to Ron. "I'm going to get lunch going."

"Mom, he knows the whole story. Besides, Ron's a total Brainiac and he's going to catch too many run-on sentences and uses of passive voice."

Ron held the paper to his side. "May I read it, please?"

"Okay, just know that it's the first time I've had something published."

"Hey, I've never had anything published," he said, then sat down on the couch next to Sierra and opened up the paper. "I like the title. I'm surprised Alice Bender let you put her photo next to Sierra's and Roscoe's."

"She's a really cool lady. When I asked her permission about exposing her personal life, she didn't blink. She thought it would be good for people to realize they weren't alone. Domestic violence can invade anyone's home. It can trap wealthy families too. There's no shame in it."

"There's shame when we look the other way. All right, be quiet now so I can read this."

### *Rescued*

### *By Casey Riley*

*I* never thought much about the financial crisis that blew through people's lives. I was fourteen years old in February 2008. I am now sixteen. I didn't think my life had been touched by it. I was wrong.

*I have a simple understanding of what caused the problem. Too many bad loans were given that could not be paid back. Debt swallowed credit. The important question now is: did we learn anything? Will we pay attention to the warning signs, or hear the alarms ring across trading floors, or behind the doors of blue chip financial firms? Can we prevent it from ever happening again?*

*We've been told the reason behind the bailout. At my young age, it makes sense to me. These companies were too big to fail. The world economy would have gone into free fall, crashed and burned, if we didn't offer a helping hand. Fair enough. But if we thought these firms were too big to fail two years ago, well, guess what? They are even bigger today. So if it happens again, should we rescue?*

*Hopefully, we won't have to decide. Hopefully, the powers that be, the people who run these nine colossal firms (which hold more than 70% of the U.S. financial system) learned to be good. Because as much as I would like my parents, and friends' parents, to be in a far better position to help again, should the need arise, I hope they will be remembered a little more this time. Because guess what? We were in need of some help too, and many still are. Of course, some might say, "You think it's bad now. Well, you'd really be crying the blues if we didn't have a taxpayer bailout."*

*Perhaps, but fair is fair. Rescue is not just about helping the big fish, while leaving the smaller ones gasping for air. It is about compassion. It means we understand that we are all connected and are willing to help, even at great cost. It is vital to keeping everyone, big and small, healthy.*

*Fortunately, there are many people who understand that compassion adds value to society and keeps it moving forward.*

*I live in the town of Riverton. It is an affluent area. People work hard for their money. Kids work hard in school so they can make money. We have our share of problems, like all towns, like all families. A few months ago, my sister wrote an article for this paper titled,* When the Hard Times Hit, the Hitting Gets Harder. *Well, the hard times hit, and it still hurts.*

*Would these times be harder if we didn't rescue? Most experts say yes. But that's not really the point, is it? Parents like mine did rescue. They weren't asked. They were told. They did what they had to do. Now, how about giving a helping hand to smaller areas beyond Wall Street, like the Riverton Family Retreat or the Riverton Animal Shelter, or to those thousands of people who are about to lose their homes?*

*But come on, those facilities aren't as important as the pillars that hold up our economy. Well, Alice Bender, and the many women she has helped, might disagree with that. Once the town slashed the budget for the family shelter, many women and children who were victims of domestic violence had to remain victims. They had no place to go. Thankfully, Alice Bender is not only financially successful, and helps put people in homes that they can realistically afford, she also recognizes the high value of compassion. She donated a large amount of her own money into that facility, and is one of the main reasons it has remained open to this day. Why? Because she knows what it is like to be on the receiving end of a closed fist. She has been a victim of domestic violence. I've seen her scars.*

*I also wear a scar. I'm looking at it as I write this piece. It is a reminder to me of the sacrifices we make for love and friendship, and how it can breathe life into a fatal situation. I took a bullet for my dog, literally. My dog was trying to protect, and then I tried to protect my dog. It worked. Sierra was not like that when I first saw her, cowering at the corner of her cage at the Riverton Animal Shelter. A facility that would soon be closed due to budget cuts from the town's economic constraints. The reason behind the decision was simple. There wasn't enough money to keep all resources in the town going. It was earmarked as non-essential. Well, I don't want to go into the grisly details, but believe me when I say, if it wasn't for Sierra, Mrs. Bender might not be here today. And if Mrs. Bender wasn't here, what would have happened to the Riverton*

*Family Retreat? What would happen to those women and children who are also in similar dangerous situations?*

*Sierra had been starved and mistreated. She was angry. She was scared. I gave her love. She saved a life. I saved hers. She changed mine.*

*There are beautiful dogs, cats, and other animals at the shelter, which is now privately owned and is a thriving community asset. It employs, it educates, it saves lives, all lives. It stays active and healthy due to the compassion and financial rescue of Peggy Kelley. She is another woman with a big wallet, and an even bigger heart, who understands that rescue and compassion have a life-saving, ripple effect.*

*So, should we rescue? Absolutely, it will spread the wealth. And that's good for man and beast.*

I went into the kitchen and set the table. Mom was putting out the sandwiches. She handed Sierra a big piece of turkey. Amazing, that same strong jaw, which could have ripped open a man's throat just a few weeks ago, is now gently licking the meat from my mom's hand.

Ron walked in. I took in his warm, lopsided grin and realized: it wasn't just Sierra, or Roscoe, Samson, or Alice Bender. It wasn't just the women and children at the Riverton Family Retreat, or all the homeless or mistreated animals. It wasn't just Cindy or Anna. I might have taken a bullet for my dog, but without Sierra, without any of them, without the shelter, without this summer, it would have taken me so much longer to believe that I had been rescued too.

*Thank you for taking the time to read this book. If you enjoyed it, please consider telling your friends or posting a short review. Word of mouth is an author's best friend and much appreciated.*

CPSIA information can be obtained
at www.ICGtesting.com
Printed in the USA
LVOW04s1650060916
503439LV00023B/523/P

9 781681 601748

# About the Author

Caroline is a librarian and a lover of "all creatures great and small." She lives north of New York City and was a working actor for many years, also writing screenplays and short plays. She enjoys hiking, hanging out with nature, and turning children, young and old, on to a good read. *Rescued* is her first published novel.

http://crimsoncloakpublishing.com/caroline-mckinley.html
https://www.facebook.com/Caroline-McKinley-923335601096389/
http://yalsa.ala.org/yals/yalsarchive/volume9/9n4_summer2011.pdf
http://www.alsc.ala.org/blog/2012/11/animals-as-teachers/